A FEAST OF DEATH

By John Penn

A FEAST OF DEATH

JOHN PENN

A CRIME CLUB BOOK

DOUBLEDAY

New York   London   Toronto   Sydney   Auckland

PENN
C. 3

A CRIME CLUB BOOK
PUBLISHED BY DOUBLEDAY
a division of Bantam Doubleday Dell Publishing Group, Inc.
666 Fifth Avenue, New York, New York 10103

DOUBLEDAY and the portrayal of a man
with a gun are trademarks of Doubleday,
a division of Bantam Doubleday Dell
Publishing Group, Inc.

Library of Congress Cataloging-in-Publication Data
Penn, John.
    A feast of death / John Penn.
        p.   cm.
    "A Crime Club book."
    I. Title.
PR6066.E496F4   1991
823'.914—dc20   90-43017
                                            CIP

ISBN 0-385-41087-5
Copyright © 1989 by John Penn
All Rights Reserved
Printed in the United States of America
March 1991
First Edition in the United States of America
1   3   5   7   9   10   8   6   4   2

A FEAST OF DEATH

CHAPTER 1

Quite apart from its unusual name, the parish church of Fairfield in the Cotswolds was no ordinary ecclesiastical establishment. In the first place it was dedicated to a little-known saint —St. Blaise; in the second, it was one of the oldest churches in England, and—if major cathedrals were excluded—one of the largest. Originally it had received its charter from King John in 1198, probably for the establishment of a small chantry chapel. Since then it had been partly rebuilt and extensively added to, so that little of the original structure could be identified. But for any serious tourist in the Cotswolds St. Blaise was a must, constituting as it did a microcosm of English religious architecture. And, thirdly, it was one of the decreasing number of livings which remained in the gift of a patron.

Located on the edge of Fairfield village, not far from the small market town of Colombury and about an hour's drive from Oxford, St. Blaise was easy to reach. There were, however, many churches and chapels in the vicinity, and as the practice of Sunday worship had declined throughout the country, so had the congregation of St. Blaise. In addition, there was a perennial shortage of clergy, and it was only to be expected that when the old vicar died of a heart attack some five years ago, no replacement could be found for him.

From the local bishop's point of view, the obvious answer was to unite three or four parishes, so that St. Blaise could remain an active place of worship, rather than a mere historic remnant which the knowledgeable could admire, the ignorant could gawp at and where the weary could rest their feet after a day of sight-seeing. This solution, however, did not endear itself to the Parochial Church Council of St. Blaise, of which—in the absence of a vicar—Lady Gerart, the senior church-warden, was acting chairman.

The Gerarts lived in Fairfield Manor. Constance Gerart was the wife of Sir William, the local Member of Parliament and the patron of St. Blaise. He himself had a minimal interest in the church and its doings, but his wife joined forces with Miss Jane Mabson, a rich spinster who was proud to have come from an old Oxfordshire family and had lived for most of her life in a nearby mansion known simply as The Hall, now much too large for her; she acted as the Parochial Council's honorary secretary.

Together the two women had sufficient influence to force Sir William—and of course their colleagues on the council—into action. Pressure was put upon the bishop, and finally he agreed that the Parish of St. Blaise should remain independent, and that, subject to Miss Mabson becoming a licensed reader—the study for which appointment could readily be done at home—non-sacramental services could be held in the church, and a priest made available from time to time for special occasions.

It was amazing what the council achieved. On Saturdays and the eves of religious festivals, the church was swept and burnished, and the sanctuary adorned with fresh flowers. And at least every Sunday there were services of prayers, lessons, hymns and a homily; Miss Mabson, once qualified, was even allowed to bless the congregation, as long as she referred to "us" rather than "you." The crypt was cleared of rubbish and redecorated, to become a parish meeting-room. Of course, it helped that money—mainly the Gerarts' and Miss Mabson's money—was no object, and that the parish could even afford to pay a verger's wages.

Naturally, the situation was not ideal. They still needed a priest and they continued to bombard the bishop with requests, pointing to the historic importance of the church. These requests were received with apologies and a promise that if it became possible and there was a suitable candidate . . .

Reluctantly the enthusiasts accepted the inevitable, and did their best. Their best was very good, and surprisingly congregations began to grow, even without a vicar, as the council never failed to point out to the church authorities. There were in fact several reasons for this growth. Lady Gerart and Miss Mabson used their not inconsiderable influence in the neighbourhood to persuade friends and acquaintances that it was their duty to support the parish church. Sir William's secretary, one David Walden, turned out to be a very fair organist, so that the fine old instrument could be rebuilt and once more put to use. And the council worked hard—and at this moment with a specific objective.

For the first time for a great many years the patronal festival of St. Blaise—St. Blaise's Day—was to become an event. Even the last vicar had failed to do more than make a casual and prayerful reference to the occasion, and in previous years the Parochial Council had been too preoccupied with survival to spare time to organize a suitable celebration. No council member could imagine the connection between a saint who, after a life of severe penance passed among wild beasts in a cave on Mount Argeus in Armenia, had eventually been beheaded in 316 A.D., and this quiet corner of the Cotswolds. To be candid, no one much cared. The church had been dedicated to this obscure saint, and he provided a day to be celebrated.

It was perhaps unfortunate that St. Blaise's Day happened to fall on February 3, when the weather was guaranteed to be abysmal and tourists conspicuous by their absence. If there was no snow, there would certainly be rain, and it was always cold at that time of year; no one in their senses would plan anything out of doors. Inside was bad enough. Flowers were scarce and expensive. The heating system in the church—still due for replacement—was erratic and, even at best, inadequate. There was always a lot of illness about, so that the recently formed choir could easily be decimated, and it was not the best time to obtain the services of a visiting priest. In fact, St. Blaise and his Day had a great deal to be said against them.

Nevertheless, as soon as Christmas was over Lady Gerart, undeterred, had persuaded the Parochial Council to allow her to appoint a small committee to formulate plans for the celebration, on the assumption that the bishop would be forced to provide a priest for the festival. The first meeting of the committee was held on a chilly day with a cutting north-east wind, but the nine men and women sitting around the Gerarts' dining table at Fairfield Manor were warm and comfortable. Coffee had been served, and they knew that once the meeting was over, at about noon, the housekeeper would bring in sherry.

Constance Gerart sat at the head of the table. Grey-haired, tall, thin, elegant, she was an old hand at chairing committees, which meant that she knew how to get her way when the matter was important, and allow herself to be thwarted with grace when it was not. On this particular committee there were only two people who might have the courage to attempt to thwart her.

One was her daughter, Veronica, aged nineteen, home from a finishing school in Switzerland and unsure about her next move. Her interest in St. Blaise and his church was negligible, and she had agreed to be co-opted to the committee merely because David Walden had been bullied into becoming its secretary.

The second was Jane Mabson, who was the opposite of Constance Gerart in appearance, being short and plump and quite indifferent to what she looked like. She didn't give a damn for anyone, but took it for granted that she would get her own way, and had to be treated with tact. Luckily, she rarely disagreed with Lady Gerart on subjects of any consequence.

Of the others, Sylvia Ashe was the wife of Simon Ashe, who was something in the City. She was almost as uninterested as Veronica, and was there because the Ashes had fairly recently bought a large house in the district, and Sylvia saw the operation as an entrée to local society. In the circumstances, it was unlikely that she would wish to oppose Lady Gerart.

Next to her sat Dorothy Brevint, married to an army colonel, who had to his annoyance been invalided out of the service because of a heart condition on the eve of what he hoped would be the year in which he was promoted to brigadier. Some years ago the Brevints had bought the old vicarage next to the church and had spent a considerable amount of money modernizing it. Mrs. Brevint was a willing worker, but unaggressive, devoting a great deal of time to her husband's well-being.

Also included, largely for the sake of democracy, were a local farmer's daughter and the owner of Fairfield's general store, neither of whom had much to contribute. Apart from the shopkeeper and Walden, the only other man at the meeting was John Courtney, a retired schoolmaster, whose initial and perhaps natural reaction had been to view the whole affair with some little cynicism.

Lady Gerart took the chair, and opened the proceedings. It had been obvious during the casual conversation over coffee that, in spite of her natural self-restraint, she was tense, perhaps excited. Only Miss Mabson, who had arrived before the others, had been let into the secret, and she was looking slightly doubtful.

"The first—indeed, the main—item on the agenda," Lady Gerart said, "is the plan for February 3—as you all know, our patronal festival, which I think we should refer to as the 'Feast of St. Blaise.' " She stared around the table, as if awaiting some religious objection to this terminology. None was offered, and she proceeded.

"But before we come to that, I have something of the utmost importance to tell you." She paused impressively. "As you may know, my husband was up at Oxford with a Bishop Payne whose diocese is in the north of England. Sir William has been taking advantage of this friendship in the interests of our parish, and this morning he received a letter from our own bishop. It seems that, thanks to the intervention of Bishop Payne, the Parish of St. Blaise is at least to have a priest-in-charge in time for the patronal festival. And there is a good possibility that after a time, when the formalities have been completed, and all the necessary approvals obtained, he may be instituted and inducted as our new vicar."

There was a general and surprised murmur of interest, of pleasure. Every member of the committee looked expectant. Even Veronica, Constance Gerart noted with some amusement and relief, was no longer gazing with starry eyes at David Walden. She waited for the questions to begin before she lifted her hand.

"I'll tell you all I know," she said. "First, he is a nephew of Bishop Payne, which of course makes him doubly acceptable to us. He's a young man in his early thirties. He's unmarried. I gather he tends to be high church, which should appeal to many of us, and rather likes to be called Father Payne."

"He sounds wonderful." Sylvia Ashe was the first to respond.

"Too good to be true, if you ask me," said Miss Mabson somewhat acidly. "There must be a catch. What is it, Constance?"

"It's not a catch, by any means." Lady Gerart spoke slowly. "It's merely a minor difficulty. Since his ordination Father Payne has spent his time as a curate in a very busy parish in the East End of London. Now, it seems that his parents are dead, and Bishop Payne is his only living relative, apart from a sister. Recently he has been compelled to take six to eight months off to look after this sister, who has been suffering from some kind of nervous breakdown. Naturally, his London appointment had to be filled, and he is now without a post. What's more, the last few months have been something of a strain for him, and it is considered best that he shouldn't be sent to too demanding a parish. So Bishop Payne, as a friend of my husband, kindly thought of us. The minor difficulty is that he must be inexperienced about what is expected of a priest in a country parish like St. Blaise."

"Does that matter?" Veronica asked.

"Poor young man," murmured Dorothy Brevint. "I think the fact that he was so devoted to his sister shows the right spirit."

"That's as may be," Jane Mabson said bracingly. "The point is, do we want an inexperienced young city curate, and one who has obviously been under some strain recently, as our parson? I hope that nervous breakdowns don't run in the family."

"I agree with Veronica," said Lady Gerart. "I don't think background matters. For one thing, his inexperience in country ways is likely to make him more—what shall I say?— malleable, and more likely to conform to our wishes about the kind of services he conducts. And there is no suggestion that he's about to break down himself," she added acidly to Miss Mabson.

"Lady Gerart, the living is still legally in the gift of Sir William, is it not?" interposed John Courtney. "So surely he and our bishop should interview the proposed new priest, with at least some representatives of our Parochial Church Council."

"You're quite right, in theory, Mr. Courtney," said Lady Gerart. "But on this occasion there's an element of urgency; we need him quickly, and Bishop Payne is anxious to get his nephew settled as soon as possible, so my husband is at this moment on the telephone, taking a poll of the council members who are not here, and we're hoping that we can agree to forego interviews. In any case, our own bishop has just gone away for some weeks, and before he went he agreed to this arrangement. I'm sure you'll agree it's a sensible step in the circumstances. After all, it's not an irrevocable appointment. He will only be a priest-in-charge. If he proves to be unsuitable . . ."

"Personally, I think we're lucky to get anyone." Sylvia Ashe supported Lady Gerart. "We'll just have to make allowances for him if he's not quite the experienced, mature man we might have liked to have."

A murmur of agreement went around the table, and only

Miss Mabson was heard to remark, "It's something of a risk we're taking, but still . . . You never know. He might well be better than someone set in country ways."

Lady Gerart was pleased. For the sake of the bishop, whom she liked, she was most anxious that his nephew should receive a warm and speedy welcome.

"Good," she said, smiling. She had saved the best news till last. She looked around the table at the faces, intelligent, dumb, slightly bored, anxious, eager to please, and added, "One could say that this was meant. The Christian name of our new vicar-to-be is Blaise, so he's The Reverend Blaise Payne. Most appropriate, don't you think?"

When the Brevints bought the original vicarage of St. Blaise, next door to the church, part of the not inconsiderable sum they paid was used to purchase a property known as Church Cottage, a small house at the far end of the lane that ran beside the garden of the old vicarage. It was an attractive place, much more comfortable than the parson's previous abode, and he was happy to move into it. Unfortunately he died soon afterwards.

Always hopeful that there would be a new incumbent, Lady Gerart and her friends had arranged for Mrs. Dolbel, who had acted as housekeeper for the widowed previous parson, to keep Church Cottage aired and dusted and generally habitable. Tom Cresford, the verger, tended the little garden and, generously paid by the Gerarts and Miss Mabson between them, took care of any necessary repairs. But any uninhabited house becomes sorrowful after a while.

The Reverend Blaise Payne—or Father Payne, as some of the council members were beginning to call him—was due to arrive on the first Friday in January. This would give him a little time to settle in before the Feast of St. Blaise at the beginning of February. Meanwhile, Church Cottage was hurriedly given a thorough spring-clean, and the central heating, which had been installed when the house was bought, put into action. The chimney in the sitting-room was swept, and the fire laid ready. Whatever the weather, the new vicar would not be cold.

Lady Gerart went to Oxford and bought curtains to replace those which had originally hung in the old vicarage, and were by now dilapidated. Miss Mabson arranged for the larder and the refrigerator to be stocked. Mrs. Ashe and Mrs. Brevint removed some poor bits of furniture and substituted better pieces. No flowers were available, but Veronica amused herself by creating a couple of elaborate arrangements with dried leaves and berries. By the Friday that Father Payne was expected Church Cottage was looking its best. Even a watery sun emerged to welcome him.

It was about half past two on that Friday afternoon when Sir William telephoned the cottage to say that Father Payne had been on the line. He would be unable to arrive in Fairfield until about five o'clock in the evening. By that time it would be dark, but Lady Gerart had sent him a map, and he expressed every confidence in finding his way to Church Cottage. It was inconvenient, but not more than that. Lady Gerart and Miss Mabson would wait to welcome him, and Mrs. Dolbel promised to stay to prepare his supper.

These arrangements organized, Mrs. Dolbel retreated to the kitchen, while the two ladies settled themselves in the sitting-room. Mrs. Dolbel brought them tea. Time passed. Five o'clock came and went. Mrs. Dolbel asked if she should light the fire. Lady Gerart firmly vetoed the suggestion.

"Where is the damned man?" She permitted her irritation to show as Mrs. Dolbel left the room. "I suppose he's lost his way."

"Presumably." Miss Mabson was also impatient.

At six-fifteen Mrs. Dolbel, full of apologies, said she would have to be getting home to make her husband his supper, but everything was ready for the vicar, and would only need warming up. She would be along in the morning.

When she had gone Jane Mabson said, "I suggest we give him till half past. If he's not arrived by then, we'll leave him a

note and go ourselves. It'll mean leaving the front door unlocked, but that can't be helped."

"Right," Constance Gerart agreed. "It's not a very good beginning, but it's not our fault."

Lady Gerart was writing the note when they heard a car
come down the lane, and stop outside the cottage. She and
Jane Mabson exchanged hopeful glances. The doorbell rang.
Together they went into the tiny hall, and Lady Gerart opened
the front door.

"Good evening, I—I'm Father Payne. I do apologize for being so late. You shouldn't have waited for me." A tall, dark
figure appeared in the doorway.

"Come in! Come in!" Lady Gerart made an effort to sound
hospitable. At least the new vicar had arrived. "We were just
leaving, but—"

"Please don't let me delay you, Lady Gerart. It *is* Lady Gerart, isn't it? And Miss Mabson?"

"Yes. How clever of you to guess!" Constance Gerart found
herself almost simpering, which was most unusual for her.
"We'll show you where everything is, then we'll go. I'm afraid
Mrs. Dolbel—she keeps the house clean, and so on—has already left, but she's cooked a meal for you, and she'll be here
in the morning. We'll meet you in the church about ten
o'clock to discuss general matters—Tom Cresford, the verger,
will come and fetch you—and then there'll be a small meeting
about arrangements for the festival. That will be all right?"

"Of course, Lady Gerart—whatever you had in mind. And
please don't apologize for anything. The delay's completely
my fault, and I assure you I'm quite capable of taking care of
myself. I should have arrived long before this, only, you see—
en route here I had the misfortune to kill a cat."

CHAPTER 2

"So what's he like, our Father Blaise?" Veronica Gerart demanded as they sat down to dinner that evening. "Tall, dark and handsome, I hope?"

She smiled across the dining-table at David Walden, who was tall and fair and, with his slightly crooked face, most appealing. Being dark herself, she preferred fair men, and she knew that she adored David. But it wouldn't hurt to disturb his complacency a little. The two of them had been lovers for three months, and she suspected that he might be beginning to take the situation for granted. For her it was an unsatisfactory long-term arrangement, and something needed to be done about it.

Jane Mabson, who had come back to the Manor with Constance to share a family meal, answered Veronica. "He's certainly tall and he's dark—the kind of man who ought to shave twice a day. But I wouldn't say he was handsome. He looked unhealthy to me—pasty-faced, as if he could do with some good fresh air."

"He's not that bad-looking," Lady Gerart said. "I thought he had rather fine eyes."

"Good God, women!" Sir William expostulated. "You're not going to marry the man. He's our new vicar. Who cares a damn whether his eyes are blue, brown, or as pink as a pig's or yellow like a gull's? What we want to know—at least what

David and I want to know—is what kind of chap he is. You say he killed a cat. Speeding, was he, in a fast car?"

"Definitely not speeding, I should think, dear," said his wife. "He drives an ancient Ford. You could hear it rattling all the way down the lane before he arrived. I can't believe it would do more than fifty with a following wind, as they say."

Sir William snorted, and David Walden inquired, "How did he come to kill the cat?"

"Apparently it was in a narrow lane," said Miss Mabson. "The animal shot out from the entrance to a field right across his path. It might have been chasing a rabbit or something. He said he didn't have a chance to stop, but he clearly felt badly about killing the poor beast."

"What did he do?" Veronica asked.

"He took it to the nearest house, but the people there said they'd never seen it before, and in the end he left it on the grass verge. What else could he do?" Miss Mabson said.

"Nothing, I suppose," replied David. "You don't have to report killing a cat, as you do with a dog if you can't find the owner."

"Doing anything else would merely have made him even later," Lady Gerart pointed out sharply. "After all, the cat was dead. There are plenty of stray cats roaming around the countryside. I nearly hit one myself the other day."

The conversation became general as the houseman came in to remove the soup plates and serve the main course. Sir William said it looked as if they were in for a busy time in this session of Parliament; he'd brought a lot of papers with him to read over the weekend, and he and David had better get down to work immediately after dinner.

"David and I will have our coffee in the study, Constance, if you and Jane will excuse us."

"Of course, dear. But you can't work all the weekend. Anyway, I'll need David tomorrow morning, if you'll spare him. I told Father Payne that we—the committee organizing the feast day—would meet him in the church at ten. There's so much to discuss, including the music and the service, quite apart from the parish lunch. And really, William, you should come along too, if only to meet him. You *are* the patron, and it would be a courtesy to Bishop Payne and the local bishop."

"Oh, very well," Sir William agreed reluctantly. "I suppose you're right. Though I must say you're not giving the wretched chap much time to settle in. He only arrived to-night, and you're going to have at him first thing in the morning."

"Hardly first thing, dear, and there's not a great deal of time before the third of next month. We won't expect too much of him, I assure you. In any case, as you know, his new bishop's away, so he can't call on him at present, though he should probably go into Oxford to see the bishop's secretary and make arrangements to meet the rural dean so that they can tidy up any administration that's required. And the next formal meeting of the Parochial Council's not till next week, either," she concluded triumphantly.

Constance Gerart, having got her way, smiled benevolently round the table. Perhaps it was fortunate that she couldn't read her companions' thoughts. Jane Mabson alone was fully in agreement with her. Sir William had decided that it might be desirable to stay up in London for a couple of weekends before St. Blaise's great day, and was wondering if Constance would accept parliamentary business as an excuse. His daughter, who had made a good guess at what he had in mind, and knew that Constance would demand her own presence at Fairfield, realized that her opportunities to be with David during the next few weeks were diminishing rapidly, and was far from pleased.

Most annoyed of all was David Walden himself. Having failed to distinguish himself at Oxford—he had narrowly missed becoming President of the Union and had acquired only a poor second-class degree in history—he had seen his hopes of a political career disappearing and had jumped at the chance to be Sir William's personal secretary. What he hadn't bargained for was to be owned—soul and body, he thought, glancing at Veronica—by the whole damned family.

That Sir William should keep him busy was reasonable, though the old man was demanding, and he sometimes wished he had a forty-hour week with set free times. But Lady Gerart also expected him to be at her beck and call, especially now that she was so preoccupied with the new priest and the so-called Feast of St. Blaise. Until he had met Lady Gerart David had never heard of St. Blaise, who seemed to him a singularly obscure and unimportant character, and very likely to have been a totally mythical figure.

And then of course there was Veronica. Very often he felt himself to be in love with the girl, but sometimes he doubted his feelings—and hers. She was young, extremely attractive, but with no particular talent. Clearly she thought it would be fun to be a "young married," but he was in no position to marry her, or anyone else. He had no money, and few prospects. The Gerarts wouldn't welcome him as a son-in-law, and if Sir William discovered he was screwing his daughter, he would be out on his ear in the time it took to pack his bag. He wondered how much he would really mind if she deserted him for Blaise Payne, and decided that, on balance, he would.

Father Payne had said goodbye to Lady Gerart and Miss Mabson with relief. He shut the front door of Church Cottage, put up the latch and attached the chain, then leant against the wall of the hall for a moment.

It had been a hard day, and he was exhausted. The cat had been the last straw. He would have liked to go to bed immediately, and sleep the clock round, but realized that he must at least eat Mrs. Dolbel's—was that the woman's name?—meal, and unpack a little. And by ten tomorrow he must be in the church, bright-eyed and ready to make a good impression on some of the more important parishioners of St. Blaise; he had no doubt that as many of them as possible would put in an appearance, if only out of curiosity. But long before that Mrs. Dolbel would have arrived at the cottage, and she mustn't think him a slob.

He heaved a sigh, pushed himself upright and passed a

hand over his face. He must concentrate, get his thoughts clear. He made himself a mug of instant coffee, twice the usual strength, and drank it black. Its first result was to make him realize how many hours had passed since he had last eaten. He started on the cheese and fruit, while the casserole Mrs. Dolbel had prepared was heating. He ate ravenously, and the food helped him enormously. He washed up the dishes meticulously.

His next task was to unpack. He hung suits in a wardrobe and put away shirts and underclothes and a few sports clothes in the chest of drawers. He kept separate the clerical garments, the clerical dog-collars and vests, the long cassocks and the surplices. He was a tidy man. The result pleased him.

Having disposed of the clothes and personal articles, including an electric razor, he opened his heaviest suitcase, which was full of books. They were mostly religious tomes of various kinds—lives of saints, with some essays and a little poetry. Among them were a number of other reference books, including a copy of Crockford's, and a few novels.

Finally he unlocked his briefcase. Apart from personal papers, this contained a Bible, a Book of Common Prayer, letters, several sermons from an agency that had obviously been well used, and a talk—about three-quarters finished—on St. Blaise, which he would have no difficulty in completing. Lady Gerart had said that they would expect only a few words from him on the coming Sunday, so there would be no need to work up a sermon immediately, which was a considerable relief. He removed the Bible, the prayer book and the sermons, before relocking his briefcase.

He put the Bible and the prayer book on his bedside table, and carried the books and the briefcase into the small room next door that was furnished as a study. He arranged the books on some shelves, but left the sermons and the draft talk on St. Blaise on the desk. He wondered if Mrs. Dolbel was a curious woman. First impressions were important.

Satisfied that he had done all he could, he had a hot bath and went to bed. By now it was after midnight. He set his alarm for seven. He would be up, dressed and at his prayers or at work when this Mrs. Dolbel arrived.

Exhausted by the events of the day, he slept heavily. But around four o'clock in the morning he stirred. Instantly he was awake. He was sweating and his heart was thumping. For a moment he thought, Dear God, I'm going to die—and how ironic it should be now, just when—

Then he sat up. His heart quietened. It had been a nightmare, nothing more. Yet, even though he was wide awake, he could still visualize the wretched cat. It had been a tabby, with markings not unlike Blodge, the pet he had been given on his tenth birthday. He covered his ears. He could still hear the beast scream as the car hit it.

He pushed back the bedclothes, staggered out of bed and turned on the light before rushing to the bathroom in time to vomit into the lavatory pan. Absurd, he thought, as the spasms eased, absurd to care so much about an animal. But he had been brought up by his father, a harsh, unforgiving clergyman, and a succession of housekeepers; he could understand why his mother had run away soon after he was born, but he had had no chance to love her. He had loved Blodge instead, and only Blodge.

He washed his face in cold water, swilled out his mouth and returned to the bedroom, but the image of the cat—both cats: Blodge and the pathetic object the car had hit that afternoon —remained with him. It was strange, he thought, how small things could affect one's life so much. He lay on the bed, hands clasped behind his head, and stared at the ceiling. It was dawn before he slept again.

Mrs. Dolbel arrived at eight-thirty to find, as she later told her husband and her friends, that the parson had already had his breakfast, and was working in his study. He shook hands, and asked her to sit down.

"I gather you're going to look after me, Mrs. Dolbel?"

"I'll do my best, sir. But I've not got as much time as I used to have. We haven't had a permanent vicar at St. Blaise for years, and I've had to make other commitments. I can't give them up just like that."

"Of course not."

"The Father couldn't have been more understanding," was Mrs. Dolbel's report.

It was agreed that she should come to Church Cottage for two or three hours a day on Mondays, Wednesdays and Fridays, to clean and do laundry and a certain amount of cooking. For this she was to be paid twenty-five pounds a week, which was more than she had expected to be offered. To some extent it would mean a rearrangement of the rest of her work but, as she assured Father Payne, this would not prove difficult as the people for whom she cared were all associated with St. Blaise, and would be happy to cooperate for the sake of the new priest or parson or vicar, as they variously called him.

All this amiably settled, Mrs. Dolbel, who was not averse to a good gossip, was happy to chat about the parish, and Father Payne acquired a great deal of more or less accurate information, which he hoped would prove useful when he came to meet his parishioners. Their talk was interrupted by the arrival of Tom Cresford, the verger. Mrs. Dolbel started on her cleaning, and Cresford took Father Payne over to the church.

Cresford, who had lived in Fairfield all his life, was proud of St. Blaise and, with the possible exception of Miss Mabson, knew more about its history and architecture than anyone. It had become part of his job to act as an unofficial guide to tourists and, though he knew there would be no tip at the end of this particular tour, he was happy to give Father Payne the full treatment.

He was expatiating on the mediaeval rood screen when the Gerarts appeared, with David Walden. There were introductions and general chatter about the church and the bishop— and, naturally, the extraordinary coincidence of names between the saint and the new priest.

"An old friend, your uncle," Sir William said cordially. "He and I were up at Oxford together, and he comes to stay from time to time. Now you're here, Payne, we must get him down

again, but we're busy men and it's not easy to fit in dates that
suit us both."

"No, I'm sure it isn't, Sir William."

"Has Cresford yet shown you what we've come to call the
'hidey-hole,' Father?" Lady Gerart asked.

And when Payne shook his head, Lady Gerart led the way
into the Lady Chapel. As David Walden went to follow the
parson and Sir William, Veronica pulled him back.

"Our Father Blaise doesn't seem too keen on Uncle, does
he?" she whispered. "Did you notice how grim he looked at
the mention of a possible visit from his dear relation?"

David grinned. "Personally I don't blame him. I met Bishop
Payne once in London, and I thought he was a fierce old boy."

"Cresford discovered it about six years ago," Lady Gerart
was saying. "We can't find any mention of it anywhere, and
we're far from certain what its original use was, but we think
it could have been intended as a safe place for the church
silver."

"We keep it in our safe at the Manor now," Sir William said
as Cresford bent down and pushed firmly at one of the stones
near the floor. Part of the wall swung slowly open to reveal a
large aperture. "Not that it wouldn't be perfectly all right here.
Not more than a dozen people know about the hidey-hole."

"The silver's mostly Victorian, but very fine," Lady Gerart
commented, "and there are some splendid Georgian candlesticks. But it'll all come out for St. Blaise's Day, Father, though
of course we'll show it to you before then."

They spent another twenty minutes in the church, by
which time it was obvious that Sir William's patience was
becoming frayed. Lady Gerart glanced at her watch, and announced that it was time for an informal meeting with those
members of the Parochial Church Council who formed the St.
Blaise's Day committee. This was to be held in the old vicarage
—the home of Colonel and Mrs. Brevint, she explained to
Father Payne. Sir William excused himself on grounds of pressure of work, and made for his car. The others, having said
goodbye to Cresford, set off on foot for the nearby vicarage.

Lady Gerart, accompanied by Father Payne, went ahead, Veronica and David following behind.

When Lady Gerart and Payne were far enough ahead to be out of earshot, Veronica turned to David. "He's really quite a dish, isn't he? I should think he'll do quite well."

"Let's hope you're right," replied David. He refused to be drawn into a comment on the new priest's appearance.

CHAPTER 3

By the end of the following week it was generally accepted that the Reverend Blaise Payne was an acquisition, and that the Parish of St. Blaise was fortunate to have him as its priest. If matins the previous Sunday hadn't proceeded quite as fluently as might have been expected, it was understandable. He would soon learn the kind of service the parish preferred. He had shown himself to be a modest man, prepared to listen to advice, prepared to be amenable to suggestion, prepared to work.

Of course, everyone was not equally enthusiastic about him. Sir William Gerart, for one, hadn't taken to him, declaring that they'd never make a bishop out of the man. Miss Mabson's original slight misgivings had returned, though she could have given no rational excuse for them. But on the whole all agreed that he had made a good beginning.

Constance Gerart's reaction to Father Blaise, at first so positive, had become slightly ambivalent. On the one hand, she was certainly pleased that St. Blaise was fortunate enough to have a priest of its own again. On the other, she would perhaps have liked him to be somewhat more extrovert and less tense, but one couldn't have everything—still less every desirable trait in any individual. In any case, his cooperation had been such that the meeting that morning to finalize arrangements for the feast day on the third of next month had gone extremely smoothly, and she had got her own way on every item that mattered. On balance the parish had done well, she decided as she strode along the path through Copley Wood with her two dogs.

Lady Gerart had been to Colombury to visit a former house-keeper of the Manor, who was seriously ill. It had been a depressing visit, and she had decided to make a detour on the way home to give herself, and the dogs, some exercise by walking through the woods for an hour or so. Her husband and David were driving down from London for the weekend, though they wouldn't arrive until around six, but glancing at her watch she now realized that it was time to return to the car and head for home. She whistled for the dogs, who had galloped off into the woods.

The dogs, a Jack Russell and a wolfhound, were well-trained and usually obedient, but on this occasion they didn't respond. Lady Gerart whistled again, then called. They still didn't appear. Impatiently she plunged off the path in the direction they had taken. A bramble snagged her stocking, and she swore under her breath. She continued to call, and finally was rewarded by the sound of heavy breathing and scratching.

She found the dogs on the edge of a small clearing. They were busy digging and, after a short pause to welcome her with barks and wagging tails, they returned to their occupation.

"Mick! Jester! Come here at once!" she ordered.

Slowly and reluctantly they obeyed, and to her horror, Constance saw something of what was interesting them so much. Protruding from the earth she saw a hand, its fingers like fat white slugs, and part of an arm. It was not difficult to visualize the rest of the body. And now the smell caught at her throat.

Constance Gerart was a disciplined woman. She swallowed hard, slipped the leads on to the dogs' collars, and pulled them away. She had seen enough to know what must be done. Making the best speed she could, she hurried to the path, and then to her car. She pushed the dogs in the back, and drove at a steady forty miles an hour to the police station in Colombury.

She found Sergeant Court struggling with paperwork, which the young constable behind the desk could almost certainly have done more easily. Court was not the most intelligent of officers in the Thames Valley Police Force, but he was the prototype of the community policeman. He had two great virtues. He had been in Colombury so long that he knew everyone in the district, and he was aware of his own limitations; he never hesitated before appealing to his headquarters.

The combination of Lady Gerart, clearly under stress, and her story of the discovery of a body in Copley Wood sent him instantly to the telephone to get instructions and request help. Hand over the receiver, he said, "Is it a male or female body, my lady?"

"I haven't the faintest idea. I didn't wait to inquire." Lady Gerart was acerbic. "As far as I know it may only be part of a body, but the remains, whatever they are, are human, and something should be done about them, promptly."

"Of course, my lady." Court glared at the constable, who he felt was smothering a laugh at his discomfiture. "Get her ladyship a cup of tea, Watkins, while I talk to Detective Chief Inspector Tansey. They're putting me through to him direct," he added somewhat pompously.

Two hours later Copley Wood, or part of it, was buzzing with activity. The Thames Valley force had wasted no time. The immediate area around the remains found by Lady Gerart's dogs had been screened, and a wide section of the surrounding wood cordoned off. Luckily the location was fairly close to the road, so that it had been possible to run cables from the generator attached to the mobile incident van, and floodlight the body. The police were at work.

Masks over their faces, two constables were slowly removing the soil around the body, and carefully depositing it on a clean plastic sheet, ready for sifting. This was not difficult. The grave was shallow, mostly formed from a natural hollow, and the ground was loose as if it had recently been disturbed. A cameraman took photographs as the work progressed. The police surgeon stood by, and the pathologist was expected shortly. The inspector in charge of the scene of crime operations issued orders. It was all unhurried, but extremely competent and experienced. Nevertheless, a murmur of distaste, disgust rather than horror, went up as the face was revealed.

To be more accurate, there was no face. The front of the head had been so battered that no features were identifiable. There was merely a pulp of dirty bone and blood and tissue. It was an unpleasant sight. The police surgeon bent over, though in this case it was clearly a formality; he had to pronounce death.

He was straightening himself as the tall, lean frame of Detective Chief Inspector Tansey came through the trees. Dark-haired and grey-eyed, Tansey was an attractive man, but his wife had left him some years ago, taking their baby daughter with her, because—or so she claimed—he was driven by ambition and devoted himself to his job to the detriment of his family life. Still in his thirties, he had become an introspective, rather lonely man, but he had mellowed recently, thanks to the influence of Hilary Greenway.

Hilary Greenway, Detective-Sergeant Greenway, had been posted to the headquarters of the Thames Valley Police at Kidlington, north of Oxford, about six months ago. She was a widow; an unsatisfactory marriage had ended when her husband was killed in the Falklands War. She had worked with Dick Tansey before, and no one dared to ask about their exact relationship. Nevertheless, everyone, from the chief constable downwards, accepted that it was close.

"A mask for you, sir," an officer said, stepping in Tansey's path, "and for the—" He stopped. He was an oldish man, and had nearly said "young lady." He corrected himself as he recognized Greenway. "For the sergeant."

They thanked him. The masks covered their mouths and noses, but in fact did little to alleviate the stench, which had become stronger as the corpse was uncovered. Gesturing to

Greenway to keep back, Tansey gave the grave a brief inspection before moving away to a safe distance. The police surgeon followed, with the scene of crime inspector.

"What can you tell us?" Tansey asked.

"Damn all, at the moment," said the doctor gruffly. He had been caught just as he was going out to dinner, and his wife had not been pleased. "You can see for yourself it's a male body, naked, and its owner is well and truly dead."

"Thanks a lot!" Tansey didn't argue, but he wasn't going to accept the police surgeon's off-handed manner without showing his annoyance. "Cause of death?" he demanded sharply. "Just what we can see?"

"I'm not certain. I can't see anyone standing still and being battered to death like that, can you? And there's a contusion at the back of the head that I don't like. You'll just have to wait for the pathologist and the PM."

Tansey still refused to be satisfied. "What about timing?"

"Again, I can't stick my neck out. Some days, perhaps. You'll have to wait, as I said."

"The pathologist's just arrived, sir," the inspector put in.

"Oh, fine," said the police surgeon. "I'll meet him on the path, and then be on my way. Good night, Chief Inspector."

The police surgeon nodded at Greenway and went off, swearing softly as he snagged the sleeve of his coat on a bramble. The inspector grinned at Tansey.

"An uncooperative bugger, that one," he said. "I could have done as well as that myself."

Tansey returned the grin. "It wouldn't be difficult, would it, Jim? Still, when he gets down to it, he's thorough and reliable, and that's what counts in the long run. I bet right now he's arranging with the pathologist to attend the PM. He's quite right to say there's no point in guessing now. We should know a whole lot more tomorrow."

"Yes, sir," said the inspector.

"I'll wait to have a word with the pathologist myself," said Tansey, "and then Sergeant Greenway and I will be off to call on Lady Gerart. You'll organize an inch-by-inch search of the whole area at first light, Inspector, of course."

"Of course, sir."

"Not that I hope to get much from Lady Gerart," Tansey remarked to Greenway as eventually they drove away, "but not many people go into the woods at this time of year, and she might have noticed something."

The front door of the Manor was opened by Sir William, who waved aside Tansey's warrant card. "Come along in, Chief Inspector." His eyes ran over Hilary. "You must be Sergeant Greenway. We were told to expect you. Let me take your coats."

"Thank you, sir."

"We're a little disorganized this evening, as you can imagine. My wife took it well, but finding that body was more of a shock than she cares to admit. She insisted on bathing and changing all her clothes the moment she came in, and she insisted that the dogs smelt and must be bathed immediately. The couple who look after us are having a busy time in the kitchen. But my wife's all right. She's merely resting now, and she'll be down when you want her."

As Sir William produced this stream of information, he was leading the way along a wide hall to a door, where he stopped and waved Hilary Greenway ahead of him. She went into a comfortable sitting-room of moderate size, which it was clear the family used when they were alone. The carpet and the fact that the television was on had disguised the sound of their approach, and Hilary was in time to see a man and a girl spring apart from each other.

Sir William introduced his daughter and David Walden. "Go and fetch your mother, Veronica. Tell her she's wanted by the police." He laughed, and turned to the two officers. "Meanwhile, sit down and let David get you both a drink."

"Thank you, Sir William, but I regret we're on duty."

"Nicely worded, Chief Inspector." Sir William gestured to Walden, who turned off the television. "However, as you're not here to arrest anyone, I'm sure it would be permitted. Anyway, we won't tell. What'll you have?"

Tansey had had a long day and now saw his hope of a pleasant weekend, free of work, disappearing. He raised no further objection and, by the time Walden had poured them drinks, Veronica had returned with Lady Gerart.

After the introductions, her opening remark was the one that, in Tansey's experience, every witness always made in one form or another. "I've already given a statement to Sergeant Court, Chief Inspector," she said. "Do you want it all over again?"

"If you wouldn't mind, Lady Gerart," said Tansey. "Try to visualize yourself walking along that path through Copley Wood, calling to the dogs who didn't come and— Take it from there. Every detail you can remember, however seemingly unimportant."

"All right. I called several times before I left the path. The dogs are usually obedient and, when they didn't respond, I suppose subconsciously I suspected that something was wrong. Anyway, I'd seen the direction they'd taken, and there was a narrow track to the left, so—"

Lady Gerart was conscientious, and she did her best to re-create the scene, as Tansey had requested. "There was a bramble that caught at my stocking. It pricked my leg, drew blood actually. I cursed and—"

Seconds passed. Everyone stared at Constance Gerart. She herself was staring at Detective Chief Inspector Tansey with a mixture of amazement and respect.

"You're quite right, Chief Inspector," she said at last. "I would have sworn I'd told Court everything if you'd not made me— Snagging my stockings was so unimportant and—"

"Constance, what on earth are you talking about? You're not making sense, dear."

Lady Gerart ignored her husband, and addressed Tansey. "When I bent down to examine my leg I saw something shiny lying on the ground beside the track. Really without thinking, I picked it up. It was a silver button. But my mind was on the dogs and I thought I could hear them. Almost immediately I found them and—and the body."

"What happened to the button, Lady Gerart?" Tansey asked gently, casually, though he knew that if she had thrown it away it might take days and innumerable man-hours to find it again in the undergrowth of the wood.

"I put it in my coat pocket," Lady Gerart said. "The coat's waiting to go to the cleaner's tomorrow. I'll fetch it."

CHAPTER 4

"Well, who'd have thought it?" said Chief Inspector Tansey as Sergeant Greenway drove them away from the Manor. "Of course the button could be irrelevant, lost by some young man carrying his lady-love into the woods for an amorous hour in the undergrowth. But that seems fairly unlikely."

Hilary Greenway laughed. "At this time of year, yes. The button hasn't been there long enough to get tarnished, and though it's pretty mild for January, it's still winter in the Cotswolds. She'd have to be a tough young lady to want to make love in that cold and discomfort. Not Veronica Gerart's idea, for one, I'd guess."

"Why Veronica?"

Greenway explained how she was sure their entrance into the Gerarts' sitting-room had surprised Veronica and David Walden in some kind of embrace. "Not that Veronica seemed in the least embarrassed, but I thought he did," she added.

"I didn't notice anything like that," Tansey admitted, "but oddly enough I did get the impression that Walden had seen that button before—or one like it. It's an expensive button—sterling, from the hallmark—and there's an engraving on it, which looks like some kind of monogram. It should be readily identifiable."

"If Walden knew what it was, why didn't he say so? It isn't necessarily significant. Anyone in the woods, walking a dog, say, like Lady Gerart, could have lost it."

"Or someone burying a body," said Tansey, "though I agree we mustn't be too hopeful. Still, as I say, it shouldn't be difficult to identify."

For a while they drove in companionable silence. Then Tansey sighed. Greenway glanced at him inquiringly.

"Sorry. I was letting my imagination run away with me. A bad thing for a detective to do, Sergeant."

"Yes, sir! But tell me—off the record," she said, knowing that Tansey liked to think aloud.

"Things that don't make sense annoy me," he said, "and this doesn't make sense. Someone killed a man, either on purpose or by accident—let's leave that question for the moment—so he's got a body to dispose of. We know it's not easy to get rid of a body, but this shows every sign of being a particularly hurried, inefficient job."

"Why do you say that? The grave was shallow, but the ground was hard before it was dug. The killer might not have had much time, or the right kind of tools."

"Why not? I'm assuming we're dealing with a local killer. Why should he have been so unprepared? Why choose somewhere so relatively close to the road, or at least close to an obvious track or path, somewhere where anyone was quite likely to walk a dog, and either find the grave or have the dog find it. The killer must have been bloody stupid."

"OK. Then he wasn't a local. He was passing through. He'd picked up a hitch-hiker who attacked him, and he killed him in self-defence. Or perhaps, less likely, the hitch-hiker flashed a thick wallet and the driver decided to grab the money. When they got to Copley Wood it seemed a good place to get rid of the body, and he seized his chance."

"If the whole thing was the result of a casual encounter, why did he batter in the face and strip the body? The only reason to destroy features and remove identification is to prevent or delay recognition, which suggests there's some connection between the victim and the killer that could lead us from one to the other. He forgot about fingerprints, too—another example of incompetence." Tansey was speaking more positively now. "It certainly rules out a casual hitch-hiker, or a tramp or anyone else who might have been knocked down and killed by a hit-and-run driver who got scared."

"People do strange things," Greenway ventured, "especially under stress."

"I know. I told you I was letting my imagination run away with me," Tansey said. "As the doctors kept telling us, we'll know more tomorrow. Better not to worry at it before."

"You make it sound like a bone," Hilary Greenway said. And then, "I'm so sorry, Dick," as she realized how inappropriate her words had been in the circumstances.

As he had expected, by noon the following day Detective Chief Inspector Tansey knew considerably more about the body found in Copley Wood, and what had happened to it. The pathologist conducting the PM had gone out of his way to be helpful, producing his usual competent and detailed report, and had also been prepared to offer what he chose to call "reasoned guesses," which in the past had often proved useful. Even the police surgeon, as if to compensate for his haste and brusqueness the previous day, had contributed some helpful suggestions.

The deceased was a male, and the cause of death was a blow to the back of the head. The time of death was about a week ago, and the face had been battered after death. The man had been tall, and aged between thirty and thirty-five. His body was well-nourished and had been scrupulously cared for, though it was a little overweight. The hands were soft and uncalloused; there was certainly no possibility that their owner had earned his living by manual labour. The nails were unbroken, suggesting that the victim had probably not put up a struggle, and had presumably been unaware that he was about to be attacked. It was surprising, in the circumstances, that no attempt had been made to erase or disfigure the fingerprints.

The jaw had been badly smashed, but at least two of the teeth had been crowned, and one had a gold filling. Clearly the man had paid regular visits to a dentist. His hair, which was dark, had been cut not long before his death. His only distinguishing mark was an old appendix scar.

"Definitely not a tramp," Greenway said as she sat across the desk from Tansey at headquarters.

"Definitely not," Tansey agreed. "Nor was he a hiker, nor a jogger. His feet were as soft as his hands. Definitely a sedentary type."

"But so far there's no indication that he reached Copley Wood in a vehicle of his own. So we must assume for the moment he was taken there, presumably by the killer. Does that suggest someone living not too far away, sir?" In the office or when others were present, Greenway was always punctilious about remembering their respective ranks.

The chief inspector nodded. "It may. But unfortunately no one who remotely fits his description—or at least as much of a description as we're likely to get—has been reported missing in the vicinity. A chap whose son has disappeared is coming over from Gloucester, but it's wishful thinking, I'm afraid—more of a wild hope or fear on the father's part than anything else. It's not his son. Nothing fits."

"What a pity."

"Yes. And the incident van's been on the phone. They think they've found the blunt instrument that battered the victim's face. It was, quite simply, a largish stone. There are quite a few lying around in the wood. This one would fit snugly into a man's hand, according to the inspector. Possible signs of blood, but no sign of prints."

"That's a great help, sir," said Greenway ironically. "Nothing else?"

"A man's handkerchief, cambric and reasonably expensive, Sergeant, presumably belonging to the victim, as it was buried with him. But it's unlikely to help us. They're sold all over the country. The killer evidently placed it over the victim's face before he bashed it in."

Hilary Greenway wrinkled her nose in disgust. "Perhaps he couldn't bear to look at the man he'd killed, sir."

Tansey was less sentimental. "More likely he didn't want to get himself spattered with blood," he replied, and added thoughtfully, "Incidentally, there's only one place around there where off-the-road parking is possible—Lady Gerart used it, and we think the killer and his victim did too. The scene of crime men have found a spot where they think the original attack took place, quite close to the parking place."

"Signs of blood, sir?"

"Yes, but no struggle, seemingly. There's a path from the site into the woods—again, Lady Gerart used it—but it's quite a long way to where the body was found. Although between them the blasted dogs have messed up most of any evidence there was, there are no obvious indications that the body was dragged along. The killer must be fairly big and strong if he carried his victim, either dead or dying, to the site of the makeshift grave."

The phone interrupted them as Greenway was opening her mouth to ask another question. Tansey raised his hand before lifting the receiver and snapping out his rank and name. He listened, scribbled on the pad in front of him and said, "Well done. You've been quick. Thanks a lot."

He turned to Greenway. "That was the Met. No make on the victim's prints in the Central Registry. And none in ours, of course. I suppose it was too much to hope for. What were you going to say, Sergeant?"

"The button, sir? What about the button?"

"Ah, I was coming to that. It's where we've had a stroke of luck. It's been identified. Someone had the bright idea that it might be connected with an Oxford club. As you know, there are innumerable clubs in the university, some of them obscure, though part of their obscurity is due to the fact that they're select and have few members. That's the kind of club we're looking for. Anyway, there's a shop in Turl Street which has these buttons specially made. Each year, a few weeks after the Michaelmas Term has started, three or four young men come into the shop and order blazers, asking for these buttons to be put on them."

"Could anyone do that?"

"I'm not sure how rigorous the check is, but I gather not. Each man carries a signed chitty." The chief inspector shook his head. "It all sounds pretty childish to me, but the chap in charge of the shop wouldn't say any more to the uniformed man who saw him. Anyway, we might be on to something, Sergeant. So get the car, and we'll take a little trip into Oxford."

The small dark shop tucked away in the Turl had been a bespoke tailor for a hundred years. Nowadays it also sold ready-to-wear garments, shirts, underwear, college ties, and times had changed to such an extent that it no longer allowed undergraduates to run up huge bills. Nevertheless, the premises themselves had been modernized only a little.

Mr. Turner, who came forward to greet Detective Chief Inspector Tansey and Detective-Sergeant Greenway, looked almost as old as the business. He was short and bent, but he bowed his head as if conferring a regal favour. "Please to come this way," he said.

They followed him into an office behind the shop, where to their surprise they found a computer terminal on a desk. Mr. Turner noticed their expressions.

"Oh, we have to move with the times, you know—move with the times," he repeated. "Now, I'm sorry I couldn't be more help to the young constable who came to see me, but there were questions of professional ethics involved—professional ethics. Tailors are rather like doctors, you know. But if you assure me it's important I think I can identify the buttons for a senior police officer, and possibly give you a name—a name, perhaps . . ." He glanced from Tansey to Greenway.

"I assure you it's important all right, Mr. Turner," said Tansey. "It could hardly be more important. We're dealing with a possible murder case."

"Murder—oh dear! Oh dear! None of the young gentlemen is involved, I hope."

"That's precisely why we're inquiring about the buttons, sir

—to eliminate any of the young gentlemen, as you call them."
Tansey's patience was clearly beginning to wear thin, so Sergeant Greenway intervened.

"First of all, what *are* the buttons, sir?" she asked. "What
does the engraving represent?"

"It's the N & A Club; it's been going for the last twenty-five
years, you know, the last twenty-five years."

"The N & A? Navy and Army?" exclaimed Tansey in surprise.

"Navy and Army? Dear me, no. Something very different, I
assure you. N & A stands for 'Nectar and Ambrosia,' Chief
Inspector." The old man permitted himself a smile. "It's not a
service club in any sense—or an intellectual one, I understand. It's a social club, a social club. Very high-powered, I
believe. Several former members are now in the House of
Lords."

"I see," said Tansey. "Now, what we want is a list of those—
members or not—who could have bought these buttons since
the club was formed."

"Ah, there you have me, Chief Inspector. You don't quite
understand. We have no list, and I'm not sure that one exists.
Although I believe that the number of members up at the
university is restricted, they continue to be members after
they go down and are thus entitled to wear those buttons if
they so wish. Now and again quite middle-aged gentlemen
will ask for a replacement when they've lost one."

"Has anyone asked for a replacement recently?" asked Tansey quickly.

"Oh no, Chief Inspector. It's not all that frequent a request.
All our garments have spare buttons supplied with them, naturally."

"I see," said Tansey again. He thought that Mr. Turner was
being devious, and a direct attack was required. "So you're
unable to help the police?"

"Oh, I didn't say that, Chief Inspector, only that I couldn't
give you a complete list of those who've bought buttons in the
last quarter century. For that I suggest you go and see the

current president of the club. He's the Honourable Hugh Gaverson."

"And where's he to be found?"

"He's a scholar of Balliol College, Chief Inspector. That's on the corner of—"

"Thank you, but I know perfectly well where Balliol is," Tansey said shortly. He added his thanks, but remarked as a parting shot that another officer might well return to take a statement.

Mr. Turner saw them to the door, and then went to the telephone. He thought that a warning might not be amiss. Mr. Gaverson was a good client, as had been his father and his grandfather before him. So Hugh Gaverson was ready and waiting for the two officers. A tall, willowy young man, his jeans and soiled T-shirt did no justice to his tailor.

"You're lucky to catch me," he said, after introductions had been made and he had cast an admiring glance at Hilary Greenway. "I'm just off to do some scene-painting for the next OUDS production."

"We'll try not to keep you," said Tansey, "but it's important we should trace the owner of an N & A Club button, which was found near the scene of a murder. He might be able to help us with our inquiries."

"You mean a member of the N & A is a wanted man? What fun! I shouldn't think it's any of our present members. They're a rather unexciting lot at the moment—not a murderer among them, I'd guess. And the club's always been quite harmless, you know—a few chaps who meet every other Sunday night in term time to have a meal allegedly fit for the gods; unfortunately the god bit doesn't always work." Gaverson shook his head sadly. "You can't depend on restaurants these days."

The reference passed Dick Tansey by and he said, "Do you have a list of present and past members, Mr. Gaverson?"

"Present, yes. And I could probably remember back a couple of years, but not further than that. The secretary keeps what records we have and unfortunately the poor fellow isn't available. He broke his hip skiing in the Christmas vac, and hasn't come up this term."

"Oh dear!" Tansey would have liked to have used a much stronger expletive. He was feeling frustrated, and Gaverson's light-hearted approach to a murder irritated him.

"We'd be grateful for any names you could give us, Mr. Gaverson," Sergeant Greenway said. "The button may be nothing to do with the case, but we need to know."

"Of course. I'll see what I can do."

The young man unfolded himself from the armchair in which he was sprawled, and leapt to his feet. He went to a desk which was covered with books and papers, and started rummaging through the drawers. One sheet of paper he seized upon almost immediately. "That's the present list," he said. "But there's something else—"

Tansey had almost given up hope when Gaverson uttered a sudden shout of triumph.

"Got it!" he cried. "I knew I had it somewhere." He gave the list of present members to Tansey, and then passed him what appeared to be a slim booklet. "It's the menu of our twenty-fifth commemorative dinner. Naturally not everyone accepted. Some were abroad. Some were busy. Some were dead. Some couldn't leave wife and family, no doubt. But there were over a hundred there, and their names and colleges are printed inside."

"That's wonderful," said Sergeant Greenway.

Gaverson gave her an approving smile. "I thought you'd be pleased."

"We shall have to take this away," said Tansey.

"I know, but I'd like it back, because of the signatures of the people at my table. Perhaps you could photocopy—"

"Of course," replied the chief inspector.

Gaverson was still standing, and now looked at his watch.

Tansey stood up too. He was content to leave. They had achieved considerably more than at one point he had expected. Tracing the members of the N & A who had been at the anniversary dinner was going to be a trying job, but it might be rewarding; a man who still wore his blazer with the club buttons was very likely to have gone to the dinner. The thanks he expressed to Hugh Gaverson were genuine.

"I can't offer you nectar and ambrosia," he said to Greenway as they walked across the quadrangle to the lodge, "but we've got to eat. Let's treat ourselves to a late lunch at the Randolph."

"That," she said, "sounds like a splendid idea."

CHAPTER 5

Chief Inspector Tansey and Sergeant Greenway had a brief drink together at the bar while the maître d' of the Randolph found them a corner table in the dining-room. The hotel was always popular, and today seemed busier than usual. The tables were close-packed, and any private conversation was precluded unless one were prepared to risk the chance of it being overheard. The officers were careful what they said.

But while they were waiting for their food to arrive, Tansey couldn't resist the temptation to take the anniversary menu of the Nectar and Ambrosia Club from the envelope that the Honourable Hugh Gaverson had provided, and study it.

Suddenly he gave a surprised exclamation. At that moment the waiter produced their soup, and Tansey hurriedly thrust the menu back into its envelope. Greenway was forced to contain her curiosity.

"What is it? What caught your eye?" she demanded, as soon as the waiter had gone.

Tansey said, "I was glancing down the list of names of those who'd been at this famous dinner, and what should I see but 'Walden, D. R. I.'? I suppose it could be a brother or relation, but"—he lowered his voice—"I'd bet it's Sir William's secretary, David Walden. If so, that young man's got some questions to answer about why he didn't react yesterday."

"He saw the button clearly?"

"Yes. Don't you remember? When Lady Gerart fetched it

everyone examined it, Sir William and the daughter and Walden. We passed it around from hand to hand. There was no question of a fingerprint. Walden must have recognized it."

"But he kept mum. Interesting. Of course, he knew where it had been found, so he might have been scared."

Tansey finished his soup. "Well, we'll see what he's got to say immediately after lunch. I'll phone first, but if he's still there, we'll go straight back to the Manor. It should be all right. He spends all of most weekends with the Gerarts, I understand."

"Duty and pleasure," said Greenway, grinning. "If Sir William didn't make him come, I dare say the attractive Veronica would draw him."

The waiter removed their plates and served the main course. For a while they talked of other things, including the holiday they were planning to spend together when they could get some leave. But, inevitably, as they continued with their meal, they reverted to what someone in the media had called the Case of the Copley Corpse.

"One good thing about the publicity we're sure to get," said Tansey, "is that the body should be identified before too long. After all, he's been buried for a week at least, if the pathologist is anywhere near right. I'm surprised there isn't a matching missing persons report already."

Greenway nodded. "Yes. He obviously wasn't poor, and he presumably had a home of some kind, and almost certainly a job. Even if he were on holiday someone would have been expecting him—unless he was going to a hotel by himself."

"If only we could have printed a photograph of his face," Tansey said regretfully. "But you can't just go round asking if anyone's seen a dark-haired man, in his early thirties, with a well-cared-for body, can you?"

"You certainly can't—not unless you expect a rude answer," said Sergeant Greenway.

A phone call confirmed that David Walden was available, and after lunch the two officers drove over to Fairfield Manor. In

the car, the chief inspector studied the names in the N & A
Club menu with more care, and commented aloud on several
that caught his eye. Among them were two members of the
House of Lords, three or four MPs—though not Sir William
Gerart—a leading barrister and various celebrities in the me-
dia and the world of arts and letters.

"A high-powered lot, as that chap Turner said," Tansey commented thoughtfully.

"Which is all the more reason why the body should soon be
claimed," said Greenway. "It's the poor, the destitute, the ones
with no family or connections, who manage to get killed without anyone caring a damn, isn't it?"

"Yes, generally, but—you're suggesting it was the victim
who owned the button, not his killer. That's only an assumption. There's no evidence either way. For that matter, I suppose both killer and killed could belong or have belonged to
this club."

"Perhaps David Walden will be able to tell us," Greenway
said optimistically. "Anyway, here we are at the Manor. And
judging from the cars outside, we're not the only visitors."

The houseman let them in, and left them standing in the
hall while he went to tell Mr. Walden that they had arrived.
He returned almost at once and showed them into the dining-
room, where they were greeted by Sir William.

"Come along," he said amiably. "We're all admiring the
church silver. Naturally it's going to get a good clean. It's been
in my safe for ages, and though it was carefully wrapped it
was bound to tarnish."

He stood back to let the two officers see the silver laid out on
the dining-room table. There were candlesticks of various
sizes, several chalices and some pieces that Tansey failed to
identify. He was, in any case, more interested in the people.

Lady Gerart performed the introductions. "Chief Inspector,
you've not met Miss Mabson, who lives at The Hall and is an
old friend of ours—and of St. Blaise's parish. I don't know
what we'd have done without her while we had no priest or
vicar; fortunately she took a course as a licensed reader, and

was able to conduct many services for us. Detective Chief Inspector Tansey and Sergeant Greenway," she said formally.

Jane Mabson offered them her hand. "This is a dreadful business," she said. "I hope you find the murderer very soon, Chief Inspector. We're a quiet, peaceful community here, and it's not nice to think of a killer around the place."

"Oh, I don't think we need to worry, Jane," said Sir William. "The man will be miles away from the district by now, won't he, Chief Inspector?"

"Perhaps, sir." Tansey glanced at David Walden. "We don't know much at the moment. The inquiry is really just beginning."

"You know Veronica, of course, and Mr. Walden," continued Lady Gerart. "But this is Mr. Courtney, who is a pillar of strength on our Parochial Council."

Tansey and Greenway acknowledged the introduction before Lady Gerart turned to the remaining man. "And last, but by no means least," she said, "you must meet our new priest— the Reverend Blaise Payne. We like to call him Father Payne."

"How do you do, Chief Inspector, Miss—sorry—Sergeant Greenway." Payne gave them both a nod as he offered his hand. "I must admit I share Miss Mabson's sentiment. The sooner you find the villain, the better for everyone."

"We're all agreed on that," Veronica said sharply.

The remark distracted attention from Tansey, and of those present only Greenway and perhaps Father Payne, who was shaking hands with the chief inspector, noticed his quickened interest.

"Blaise?" Tansey said. "I must admit I'm a little confused. Is there any connection between you and St. Blaise?"

The parson smiled, but he took his time answering. "None at all, as far as I know, Chief Inspector. It's pure chance. I wouldn't claim to be a saint but, yes, my first name is Blaise. That's what I was christened. The good people here seem to take the coincidence as a happy omen."

"Let's hope it will be," Tansey said pleasantly. "You were at Oxford, I believe, as was Mr. Walden?"

"Yes, but not at the same time, or college, as Mr. Walden. I was up about ten years earlier, I think." Payne smiled again.

"But you were both members of the N & A?"

"The N & A?"

"The Nectar and Ambrosia Club, Mr. Payne. You can't have forgotten it, surely. It seems to have slipped Mr. Walden's memory, but—"

"What on earth's the Nectar and Ambrosia Club?" Miss Mabson interrupted, to the chief inspector's annoyance.

Surprisingly, it was John Courtney who answered. "It's a rather exclusive Oxford drinking club, isn't it?" he said. "We had the same sort of thing at Cambridge."

"A drinking club?" said Lady Gerart.

"It was a dining club, a social club—not just a drinking club," David Walden broke in hurriedly. "But that's not the point. The chief inspector's playing games with us. It's about that damned button you found in the wood near the body, Lady Gerart. I recognized it the moment I saw it, and I suppose I should have said so. I don't know why I was so stupid, but somehow in the circumstances it seemed best to keep my mouth shut."

"You mean it's your button, David?" asked Sir William.

"No, sir. It is not. I checked as soon as I could. All my blazer buttons are intact. I've not lost one. Would you like to see my blazer, Chief Inspector?"

"Yes, please," said Tansey bluntly, and Walden flushed.

"I'll get it," he said.

As he hurried from the room there was an uncomfortable pause, which no one seemed inclined to break. Lady Gerart and Miss Mabson began to wrap up the silver as if they needed something to occupy them. Veronica and the men looked on with seemingly studied indifference, and Sergeant Greenway, standing in the doorway, watched everyone closely.

Walden returned very quickly, carrying a dark blue blazer which he held out to Tansey. "Here you are, Chief Inspector. It puts me in the clear, I should guess. All buttons as they should be."

Tansey passed the blazer to Greenway, who examined it with some care before returning it to Walden. "That's fine," she said non-committally.

Suddenly Veronica intervened. "What about Father Payne?" she demanded. "Aren't you going to ask him to account for all his buttons?"

"Veronica!" Lady Gerart was shocked.

The priest laughed before anyone else could intervene. "I couldn't—account for my buttons, I mean. It's years since I possessed an N & A blazer. I'm afraid my interest in the club has waned."

"But you attended the twenty-fifth anniversary dinner, Mr. Payne," said Tansey.

There was a slight pause. Then, "You *have* done your homework, Chief Inspector," the parson said. "But an anniversary dinner is a little different from continuing to wear a club blazer, wouldn't you think?"

Tansey was prevented from answering by David Walden, who said, "I never saw you at the dinner, Father, but of course there were a lot of people there."

"Come to that, I never saw you either, David." Father Payne had regained his aplomb. He went on, "Anyway, if you think my non-existent button is at all relevant to your case, Chief Inspector, may I point out that I only arrived in Fairfield the Friday before this unfortunate man's body was discovered, and I understand it had been in the ground some time."

"Not as long as has been suggested," said John Courtney unexpectedly.

Everyone turned to him and, pleased to be the centre of interest, he paused. He was in his late sixties, a man who felt he had never received the recognition he deserved. He was glad to have retired from his teaching post in Reading, but he remained conscious of not really belonging to Fairfield. He got on well enough with everyone. He liked the villagers, but he was not one of them. Nor did he fit with the landed gentry of the area—people like the Gerarts and Miss Mabson—whom in his heart he despised. And he knew, without a shadow of doubt, that he was the most intelligent person in the room. He smiled thinly.

"What makes you say that, Mr. Courtney?" Tansey asked. "You've some information for us, obviously."

"Not exactly information, Chief Inspector," Courtney said, "but I know Copley Wood extremely well. It's a very interesting area, botanically speaking, so I often walk there, and it happens I was in that part of the wood where Lady Gerart found the body early on the previous Friday afternoon. I can assure you there was no body there then."

Tansey stared at him. "How could you possibly swear to that, Mr. Courtney?"

"I was searching all over the area the police have cordoned off. I was peering at the ground. I had my stick, and I was moving aside brambles and dead leaves and bits of branches. I would certainly have noticed a quantity of freshly turned earth."

"What were you looking for, Mr. Courtney?" Veronica said, eyes wide in amazement.

Courtney laughed. "It's quite simple, Miss Gerart. Wild violets of a special variety. I've found them in Copley Wood as early as January, but they seem to be late this year."

"Why have you held back this information? Why didn't you tell us before, Mr. Courtney?" asked Tansey.

"I tried to soon after the police arrived. I went along specially. There was a constable standing by what I think you call a mobile incident room or van or something, but the policeman wasn't interested. He took me for a sightseer and told me to move along. So I did."

Tansey nodded, though he doubted Courtney's version of what had happened—and this made him suspicious of the man's entire story. Nevertheless, the afternoon had not been wasted; it had yielded some most useful insights. "I suppose you didn't see any sign of the silver button," he said.

"No!" Courtney was firm. "And I very much doubt if I should have missed it," he added with satisfaction.

Fifteen minutes later Chief Inspector Tansey and Sergeant Greenway took their leave. Miss Mabson remained, but the other visitors, the Reverend Blaise Payne and John Courtney, left the Manor at the same time.

As the front door closed behind them, Payne said, "If I might have a word with you, Chief Inspector . . ."

"Yes, of course," said Tansey.

Courtney, feeling himself dismissed, said good afternoon gruffly, and stumped off to his old Ford, though he still looked pleased with himself.

"My car's almost as ancient as his," Payne said. "I had a rather nice coupé, but I thought it might not be quite the thing for Fairfield, so I sold it."

"Really?" Tansey didn't believe that Payne wanted to talk about cars.

"And I was right, Chief Inspector. The Parish of St. Blaise expects its parson to be high-minded and low-living. Which is why I was reluctant to admit that I had been at that anniversary dinner. Lady Gerart would consider it appropriate for David Walden, perhaps, but not for a clergyman, if much drinking was involved. And that was the impression that was given. I'm sure you understand, Chief Inspector? I'm still only the priest-in-charge here, you know. My appointment as vicar has yet to be confirmed, and that could take time—years, even. I don't want to put up a black if I can help it."

"Very reasonably, Mr. Payne." Tansey was bland. "Please don't worry about it." But once he and Greenway were alone he commented, "Odd! There were at least three or four prelates at that dinner, doubtless all drinking merrily. It was chance, and the fact that his first name was Blaise, that made me remember him from the list. Why should he be so touchy about being there?"

Greenway said, "It's quite reasonable that he wouldn't want

any suggestion of frivolity to get around when he's just come to a new job, isn't it?"

Tansey shrugged. "I expect the whole thing's irrelevant. Anyway, if Courtney's telling the truth, we've got an earliest time for burial, if not death."

"You think he might be lying?"

"He didn't exactly convince me, for a variety of reasons. He might be trying to cover for himself. And Walden wasn't very convincing either, was he?"

"His blazer buttons were all intact, but several had been sewn on non-professionally, as it were, and if he lost one by the body he's had plenty of time to sew on a spare, assuming he had one."

Tansey laughed. "Ah, I thought you'd notice something like that. That's why I passed you the blazer. Incidentally, I've not forgotten your idea that the button may have belonged to the victim. We shall have to consider that seriously."

CHAPTER 6

It was Monday morning. Mrs. Dolbel was busy dusting and vacuum-cleaning the sitting-room in Church Cottage. She was humming to herself, and wondering what she would cook to leave for Father Payne's supper when she was startled by a cry from the kitchen. She dropped the duster, and ran.

She found the parson at the sink. He was holding his right hand under the cold tap, and blood was mingling freely with the running water. For one dreadful moment the thought flashed through her mind that the priest had cut his wrist, but then she saw the nasty gash across the back of his hand.

"Oh, Father, what have you done?" she exclaimed.

"Nothing serious, Mrs. Dolbel," he assured her. "I was just trying to open this box of cereal, and I dropped the knife on the floor. I bent down to pick it up with my other hand and it slipped. It was careless of me. Stupidly I seem to have taken a slice out of myself."

"Oh dear! Let me look. You shouldn't try and open packets with a knife of that kind, Father."

"No, Mrs. Dolbel," he agreed meekly. "Meanwhile, it's beginning to stop bleeding. Do you think you could find a suitable bandage for me? I don't think a bit of sticking plaster will be adequate. I'm going to Oxford this afternoon."

"And the last thing you want is an infected hand, Father, especially with the feast approaching."

Mrs. Dolbel bustled away, and returned with a clean towel,

some antiseptic and a bandage. She dressed the cut quickly and efficiently. "There," she said when she had finished, "that should be all right for now, Father, but take care. Don't go knocking it against something, or it'll start to bleed again. I'm not sure it shouldn't have a stitch or two."

"Leave it, Mrs. Dolbel. I'll be careful," he promised, "and thank you very much."

But Mrs. Dolbel had more to say. "It's a nasty wound, Father. If I was you, I'd not drive into Oxford today. I'd go to Dr. Band's surgery in Colombury. Get him to have a look at it. It would only take him a minute to put in a stitch."

The parson was patient. "I'm sure you're right, Mrs. Dolbel, but I've got to go to Oxford this afternoon. The bishop's secretary phoned, and asked me to call in at his office in North Hinksey and, apart from church matters, I've business of my own in Oxford that I've been putting off for days. Maybe I'll look in on Dr. Band on my way back."

Satisfied with this, Mrs. Dolbel returned to her chores and Payne retired to his study. The bandaged hand proved more incapacitating than he had expected. It was difficult to sort through papers, and almost impossible to write. Silently he cursed his carelessness. A little later, when Mrs. Dolbel brought in the post, which consisted of one letter, it took him a full minute to open it and extract the single thick sheet.

The letter was from his uncle, Bishop Payne. It was a friendly note, expressing the wish that his nephew was settling in as the priest-in-charge of St. Blaise, and hoping to hear in the near future how he liked Fairfield.

Naturally, the bishop explained, he was anxious to visit his good friend, Sir William Gerart, as well as his nephew as soon as possible, but unfortunately would not be able to be with them on St. Blaise's Day, or in the nearer future. He was extremely busy at present, and he had been asked to undertake almost immediately an extended tour of certain African dioceses with which his own diocese was associated. He was writing a letter of explanation to Sir William.

Detective Chief Inspector Tansey had not been idle over the weekend. He and Sergeant Greenway had again been in touch with Hugh Gaverson at Balliol, and had traced the present whereabouts of the secretary of the Nectar and Ambrosia Club, who had broken his hip skiing. A telephone call to the clinic in Switzerland where he was still being treated had elicited the fact that all the papers relating to the club were at his mother's house in London. More phone calls, and his brother, who was due to visit Oxford, had volunteered to find them and deliver them to the headquarters of the Thames Valley Police in Kidlington.

They had arrived that Monday morning. In the meantime Sergeant Greenway and another officer had started to check on those members of the N & A who had attended the anniversary dinner. It was tedious and time-consuming work. They were only three-quarters through their task when the records were delivered.

"Any luck so far?" Tansey asked as Greenway brought a box file into his office.

"No, sir. It's a trifle complicated, as we're looking both for someone who could be the body, and someone who could be the killer. Anyway, we decided the first thing to do was get a line on the present addresses and occupations and details of as many of these N & A characters as possible. So far we've been able to track down about forty members who appear to be all hale and hearty. But some don't answer the phone numbers we've got for them, and others are said to be abroad on business or holiday anywhere from the south of France to Tokyo. There are about thirty we haven't had time to tackle yet."

"Yes, I appreciate the problems," said the chief inspector. "Go on and do what you can, and eventually we'll get out requests to the various concerned forces to make further inquiries. And cheer up. There'll be a whole lot more names in this lot, but I'll look through the papers myself first."

Ten minutes later he exclaimed aloud. The president of the Nectar and Ambrosia Club eleven years ago had been one John Peter Courtney. And that, Tansey thought, would make him about thirty-two at the present time—ideal for the body. Of course John Peter didn't have to be related to John Courtney, the ex-schoolmaster now living in Fairfield, but it was a fairly unusual name and an odd coincidence. Tansey remembered that the older John had known that the N & A was an Oxford club.

John Peter had not been present at the anniversary dinner. Against his name on the list of invitees, which was among the papers in the file, was written "No reply." But there was an address for him, and a phone number. Tansey decided to take a hand in the checking himself, and prodded at his keypad. He listened to the ringing tone for some time, experiencing some of Hilary Greenway's frustrations. He was about to give up in disgust, when suddenly a woman's voice said, "Hello!"

"Hello," Tansey said, giving only his name. "I'm trying to get in touch with a Mr. John Peter Courtney. It's a business matter, and rather urgent. Is he there?"

"Peter? No," the voice said sharply.

"Will he be back soon?"

"I hope not! Why?"

Tansey decided there was nothing for it but to make the inquiry official. He said, "This is the Thames Valley Police Force. Detective Chief Inspector Tansey speaking. Who is that?"

"Police!" There was a pause. "My name's Ward. All right. Peter was living here until a month ago. Then, if you want to be blunt, he walked out on me, the bastard—at the end of last term, it was. He said he couldn't stand teaching any more, not at a comprehensive."

"Do you know where he went?"

"No! And I couldn't care less. I wouldn't have him back if he begged me. He was a bastard, as I say. He—"

Tansey listened patiently to the lengthy tirade that followed, and felt a certain sympathy for John Peter. Finally he interrupted, "Mrs. Ward—"

"*Miss*, or 'Miz' if you prefer. But definitely *Miss*—and that's what I intend to remain!"

"Yes, I see." Tansey wished that Greenway were dealing with this phone call. "Can you tell me if Mr. Courtney has any close relatives—father, brother, say?"

"He was an only child, as you'd expect. Spoilt from birth. His mother lives in Tonbridge. I've never met her, but I believe she's old and frail. His father's dead."

"Thank you, Miss Ward."

"Oh, and he's got an uncle living in the Cotswolds somewhere."

"Thank you again," Tansey said, and thought that he'd have no trouble tracing John Peter's uncle.

Indeed, John Courtney answered his telephone immediately, and raised no objection to coming into Oxford that afternoon. Giving the excuse that he must take a formal statement about Courtney's botanical activities in Copley Wood, Tansey arranged to meet him at the police station in St. Aldate's at four o'clock.

The Reverend Blaise Payne drove slowly and carefully towards Oxford. Luckily, his first destination, the Diocesan Church House and its associated offices, was located in North Hinksey, a mile or two west of the city, and thus almost on his way.

As he drove, he regretted the sports car he might have been using. It had been ludicrous to exchange it for this old wreck in order to avoid giving the parochial council a bad impression. The money differential would certainly be very welcome; he thought of it with pleasure. But there should have been a better compromise. It hurt his hand to hold the wheel steady while he changed gears, and he was glad to reach his first destination and rest it for a while.

His interview with the bishop's secretary dealt mainly with routine administration, and presented no problems. The bishop himself would of course wish to welcome him to the diocese when he returned some weeks hence. In the meantime, the responsible rural dean, based in Charlbury, would be in touch. Payne parted from the secretary with mutual expressions of good will, and drove on into the city.

It was years since he had been in Oxford. The place looked dirtier, busier and more commercial than he remembered. He got lost, in the one-way system, like all new visitors to the place, and had great difficulty finding anywhere to park. Finally, he managed to slip into a slot in Broad Street opposite the gates of Trinity. He left the car, making sure it was properly locked, though he couldn't imagine any self-respecting car thief wanting to make off with it, and went on foot to a nearby bank.

He had made an appointment with the manager, and was quickly shown into his office. He passed over the letter of introduction he had brought with him, was informed that his account had been transferred some days ago from the northern branch, and asked for his balance. When this information was given him, he was gratified to see that it was considerably more than he had expected. He left the bank on the best of terms with its manager.

From the bank he went to a tailor's, where he bought a sports jacket, two pairs of slacks and a suit. He explained that he had lost weight recently, and needed to replenish his wardrobe. He paid by cheque, apologizing for his bandaged hand and, since he was unknown in the shop and the amount was way above a cheque card limit, referred the assistant who had served him to the bank manager. It amused him when the man came back, smiling with pleasure, and pressed him to add some shirts to his purchases. Laden with his purchases, he returned to his car and locked everything in the boot.

While he was in the shops the weather had deteriorated and it had become considerably colder. Father Payne turned up his coat collar and set off towards Carfax. He was feeling pleased with himself. The afternoon's expedition had been a success. Thinking of his purchases, he wended his way through the crush of pedestrians up Cornmarket Street. His pleasure was short-lived.

"Billy! Hi, Billy!"

At the cry Blaise Payne stopped so abruptly that a young girl wheeling a pram close behind him pushed it into his legs. He smothered a curse. There was a moment of confusion. The girl was full of apologies, though it hadn't been her fault. Payne just managed to be polite to her.

"Billy dear! I hope you're pleased to see me," said the woman who had accosted him.

She was about thirty, small and slight, red-haired, and had pale skin with a dusting of freckles, bright blue eyes and a scarlet slash of a mouth. Her coat was the same colour as her lipstick, but the long scarf wound round her neck was shocking pink. She stood in front of the Reverend Blaise Payne, barring his way and smiling broadly.

"Kay!" he said. "What on earth are you doing here?"

"That's not much of a welcome, Billy."

She put her hands on his shoulders, reached up and kissed him on the lips. As she did so he saw John Courtney on the opposite pavement. And Courtney had seen him. Courtney had moved to the edge of the kerb and was clearly about to cross the road as soon as the traffic allowed. It would be impossible to avoid him.

Payne gripped Kay by the upper arms. "For God's sake," he said. "Try to behave yourself. A member of my parochial council is approaching fast."

There was no time for her to reply before Courtney reached them. "Hello, Father Payne," he said. "I saw you from across the street. Been shopping?"

"Hello, Mr. Courtney. Yes—shopping, the bank, the usual bits and pieces."

"And this charming young lady?" Courtney made no attempt to hide his curiosity.

Before Payne could speak, Kay said, "I'm Katherine Payne, Mr. Courtney, usually called Kay." She held out her hand.

"A relation of Father Payne?" Courtney asked.

She opened her eyes wide. "His sister," she said.

"Ah," said Courtney, "we heard you have been unwell. I hope you are fully recovered."

Kay hesitated, and then said, "More or less, thank you, Mr. Courtney. I've just come to spend a few days with my brother to complete the cure."

"I see," replied Courtney. "Well, welcome to Oxford—and to Fairfield." He paused for a moment, and then added, "I'm on my way to see the police. I have to make a statement about my search for violets in Copley Wood."

Payne nodded. "Yes, we must be off, too. We're blocking everybody."

This was a justified remark. The pavement was fairly wide here, but the three of them formed an obstruction and were causing other pedestrians to walk around them and even step into the gutter. Payne put his hand under Kay's elbow, but she held her ground.

"Search for violets?" she exclaimed.

"Your brother will explain, Miss Payne. Goodbye. Nice to have met you," said Courtney. "Goodbye, Father."

"Oh, I'm sure we'll meet again, Mr. Courtney, but goodbye for now," Kay said, smiling.

The Reverend Blaise Payne did not smile.

CHAPTER 7

The chief inspector was annoyed. He had arranged to meet John Courtney at four o'clock at the St. Aldate's police station in Oxford. It was now twenty minutes past four, and the man had still not arrived. The time Tansey was wasting could have been put to better use. He fumed. Eventually he telephoned headquarters at Kidlington, thinking that Courtney might perhaps have misunderstood the arrangements for the meeting, but was informed there had been no sign of him there.

It was half past four when a uniformed constable came into the inspector's office where Tansey was waiting, to say that Courtney had turned up at last, and had been put in an interrogation room. The chief inspector collected his papers and went along the corridor, accompanied by the constable.

"Good afternoon, Chief Inspector," said Courtney, making no attempt to apologize for his late arrival.

"Good afternoon," Tansey replied shortly. "I was expecting you at four, Mr. Courtney." He placed his files on the bare table and seated himself opposite Courtney, leaving the constable to stand by the door.

"I had a puncture, and thus a wheel to change. Then I ran into Father Payne in Cornmarket Street; he was with a young woman who claimed to be his sister."

Tansey stared at him curiously. "Have you any reason to doubt her?"

Courtney smiled. "Not really. Anyway, it's none of my business."

"Quite," said Tansey, who was beginning to dislike John Courtney. He took a typed sheet of paper from one of the files, and said, "Mr. Courtney, I thought it might save time if we prepared a draft statement of what you told me about being in Copley Wood searching for violets on the Friday afternoon a week to the day before a man's body was found there. This is based on notes taken by my sergeant at the time of our first interview, but of course you are at liberty to amend it as you wish. Would you read it carefully, please. If you find any errors, we'll have it re-typed at once."

Courtney read it through quickly. "That's fine," he said. "Very accurate and succinct."

He took the pen that Tansey offered him and signed his name with a flourish. Tansey witnessed the signature and glanced at the constable, who came forward and signed below the chief inspector as a second witness.

"This is all very formal," said Courtney.

"It could be important, sir." Tansey slipped the signed statement back into the file, gave a carbon copy to Courtney and nodded to the constable that he might leave them. "Thank you for your cooperation."

Courtney rose to go, but Tansey put out a hand to stop him. "One moment more, please. Before you leave I have a few questions that have arisen from our latest inquiries." He paused, and then asked suddenly, "When did you last see your nephew, John Peter Courtney?"

Courtney stared at him. "What the hell—?"

"I'm sure I don't need to repeat the question," Tansey said mildly.

"No, but—I don't understand. I haven't seen Peter for over a year, when I was last in London. He lives there, you know, shares a flat with some woman. They're not married, but the young don't seem to mind much about such niceties these days."

"Would it surprise you to learn that your nephew has given up his teaching job, and is no longer living with Miss Ward?"

"Not particularly. He's always done what he wanted regardless of anyone else's feelings. What I can't imagine is how you know so much about him, or why you should want to."

Tansey paid no attention to the implied question. He said, "You don't seem very fond of him, Mr. Courtney."

John Courtney shrugged. "We're not close. We exchange cards at Christmas. I send him a small cheque on his birthday. That's about all. If I go to London we might have a meal together. He hasn't been to Fairfield for ages."

"You say you send him occasional cheques. Does he have any money of his own?"

"What he earns, plus an allowance from his mother. When she dies he'll come into quite a lot. My brother went into business, and was far more successful than I ever was." Courtney couldn't hide his resentment. "But you haven't answered me, Chief Inspector. Why do you want to know all this about Peter?"

Tansey scarcely hesitated. "Mr. Courtney, I don't want to worry you without cause, but there is a possibility—and I stress that it's only a possibility—that your nephew may be dead."

"What! How?"

Either Courtney was a fine actor or he was completely innocent, Tansey reflected. "Mr. Courtney, it *is* only a possibility, as I said, but I'd like you to come to the mortuary with me, and see if you can identify a body."

John Courtney made an inarticulate sound of surprise, and Tansey watched the Adam's apple in his throat move up and down as the old man swallowed. But he recovered himself quickly, and showed he was no fool.

"You mean—the body Lady Gerart found in Copley Wood? It could be Peter?"

"I'm hoping you can tell us whether it is, Mr. Courtney."

"Very well." As Tansey stood up, John Courtney pushed back his chair with unnecessary force and got to his feet. He straightened his narrow shoulders. "I'm ready, Chief Inspector," he said with a nonchalance that was obviously an effort for him. "Shall we go?"

Detective Chief Inspector Tansey had returned to headquarters and was reviewing the case with Sergeant Greenway in his office. For both of them it had been a long, frustrating day, and little had been achieved. It was a kind of day not uncommon in their profession, but that made it no easier to bear.

John Courtney had denied that the body he had been shown at the mortuary was his nephew's. His denial had been quite definite, though he could give no convincing reason for it. Unwillingly he had provided the address of his sister-in-law, John Peter's mother, warning that Mrs. Courtney was in a nursing home and could be of no help. This had been confirmed by the matron of the home; Mrs. Courtney was far too frail to travel, and her sight was poor, so that in the circumstances identification of someone who might be her dead son was out of the question. However, Miss Ward, John Peter's erstwhile girlfriend, had reluctantly agreed to come and view the body.

"I shall be disappointed if it's not John Peter," Greenway said. "It would be so neat and tidy."

"Too neat and tidy, I expect," said Tansey, "though it would be interesting to see Mrs. Courtney's will. If her son predeceases her, who's the heir? Uncle John? But this is all supposition. What we need is a positive identification. Admittedly John Peter seems a fair bet at the moment, but—"

"There are others, sir. There's a man called Roy Belham. He's on a sabbatical year from Sussex University, where he teaches politics and economics. He was a member of the N & A Club at the same time as the Reverend Blaise Payne. He's meant to be on a cycling trip through England, researching into what life in the UK is really like, or some similar sociological topic, but his family haven't heard from him for weeks. They admit that's not unexpected, however, and say he's a pretty vague character. And there's a friend of David

Walden, who's said to be the entertainments director on a cruise ship; I've not managed to contact him yet."

"They sound long shots. Forget them!"

"What? What, sir?"

"I mean forget them for today. We've had enough, Sergeant. There is a limit, even for a Monday. Let's hope tomorrow will be better."

The Reverend Blaise Payne had no such hope. As he drove back to Fairfield with Kay beside him he was in the blackest of moods. The afternoon, which had started so well, had ended in his disastrous meeting with Kay. He glanced sideways at her, and felt anger stir in him as he saw her secret smile.

He could guess what she was thinking. He knew why she was so pleased with herself. It wasn't chance that had brought her here. She had been deliberately searching likely places for him, and Oxford represented a reasonable guess as to his whereabouts. It was a most unfortunate coincidence that had brought her to the city and to Cornmarket Street at that precise moment. She would make his life infinitely more complicated. He could already imagine the gossip she would rouse in Fairfield, whose inhabitants would expect their parson to be as pure as driven snow. His sister, indeed!

In spite of her remark to Courtney that she was about to spend a few days with him, he had tried his best to persuade her to stay in Oxford, but she had refused. Nothing would satisfy her, except that she should be with him. And he couldn't very well tell her to go to hell.

In the end, he had been forced to agree that she should come to Fairfield and to Church Cottage, but he was fearful of the consequences. To some extent—as long as he didn't annoy her—he could depend on her discretion, but she was fallible. An accidental slip of the tongue, a careless comment, and then . . . It was infuriating, when everything was going so well.

"Here we are, Kay," he said as they turned down the dark lane that led to the cottage, trying to sound cheerful. "At least we'll have a few hours to ourselves before you need to be the parson's loving sister."

He was wrong. A shadowy figure was standing by the gate. It was Mrs. Dolbel, who waved violently as they drew up, and at once came to the window of the car. "Father, it's old Mr. Finner, who lives up in the cottage at The Hall. He was gardener there for years, and Miss Mabson let him stay on when he retired. He's dying. His daughter's with him, and Dr. Band, but he's asked for the parson."

"All right, Mrs. Dolbel. I'll go as soon as I can!" Payne got out of the car.

"It's best you hurry, Father. He's sinking fast. They've been trying to ring you all the afternoon, and when your phone didn't answer they tried me." Mrs. Dolbel was eyeing Kay with interest, but it was too dark for her to get more than an impression of the figure in the front seat. "Old Tobias Finner's not really one of your congregation; in fact, I doubt if he's been near a church in years. But he's demanding the parson, as he says, and he wants to see you alone with the doctor. I came round because I thought something might be wrong. I expected you back from Oxford before now." There was reproach and curiosity in her voice.

"There's nothing wrong, Mrs. Dolbel. Now, may I introduce my sister, Miss Payne, who's come to stay with me for a few days. Kay, this is Mrs. Dolbel, who looks after me."

"How do you do, miss." Mrs. Dolbel was clearly nonplussed. "Father said nothing about a visitor. I've not made up the bed in the guest room, nor nothing."

"Please don't worry, Mrs. Dolbel. I can easily do that for myself." Kay was at her sweetest. "I'm sorry to arrive so unexpectedly."

"Yes, miss," Mrs. Dolbel said doubtfully. Then, to Father Payne, "But what about old Mr. Finner?"

"I'll be right along, Mrs. Dolbel, I promise." Payne was reassuring. "You go off home now. We'll see you on Wednesday."

"Yes, very well, Father. Good night. Good night, Miss—er—Payne."

Mrs. Dolbel mounted her bicycle and rode off. Payne had already opened the front door of the cottage. He unlocked the boot of the car and, with Kay's help, started to unpack the various purchases he had made.

"Do you really have to go and see this old geezer?" Kay asked.

"Yes, I suppose I do, though God knows what he wants—not the consolation of religion, apparently, from what Mrs. Dolbel said. And you'll really have to make up the bed in the spare room, and make sure it looks as if it's being used."

Kay laughed. "Whatever you say, Billy dear," she said.

"Good. Have a drink and make yourself at home. Mrs. D. should have left some food ready. I shan't be long, I hope."

Tobias Finner's daughter opened the door to him, her eyes red with weeping. "Oh, I'm glad you've come, Mr. Payne. The doctor says he can't last much longer, and he won't die easy unless he's seen you. I can't imagine what he's up to," she added, unconsciously echoing Mrs. Dolbel. "He's not been to church for years—says he doesn't hold with it. But he insists on seeing you and the doctor together, and the doctor's been so good, waiting around."

"Don't worry, Miss Finner. Maybe he's decided he wants a priestly blessing before he dies," Payne said, as he followed the daughter's fat legs up the narrow stairs. "People do, you know. He may even feel he's something to confess."

"Heaven knows what. He's been a good man. He was a good husband, and a good dad, and he's never done no wrong."

"I'm sure he hasn't, but you never know what may be on the mind of someone approaching his Maker."

The daughter grunted unbelievingly as she ushered Payne into the bedroom. "Here's the parson at last, Dad. Mr. Payne from St. Blaise's Church."

It was a small room, furnished functionally, but with no thought for comfort or colour. The old man, who was propped up on pillows in the middle of the big double bed which occupied much of the available space, was small too. The only sound was the buzzing of the gas fire. The room was hot, very hot. It smelt of sweat and urine and approaching death.

Tobias Finner's face was grey and drawn. He hardly seemed to be breathing. Indeed, it was possible to think him already dead until he opened his eyes, which, faded and rheumy, were nevertheless still full of intelligence.

As Payne came in the doctor, who had been sitting beside the bed, pushed back his hard upright chair and rose to greet him. Finner misinterpreted the movement, and put out a hand to stop him. "No, Dr. Band, stay, please! You and the parson, that's what I said. But you go, Jenny," he said to his daughter. "I don't want you here."

Jenny grunted again, but obediently left them. Band contented himself with a gesture, half of welcome, half of apology for the old man, and Payne nodded in return. There was a second hard-backed chair in the room, and he drew it up on the opposite side of the bed from the doctor. He sat down and they waited.

After a full minute Tobias Finner said, "I know who buried that body in Copley Wood."

Neither the doctor nor the parson spoke.

"I saw him. I was collecting twigs and suchlike for the fire. I try to do my best to help, and I was well that day," the old man continued.

"You actually saw someone burying a body?" Dr. Band said.

"No, but I saw him come back along the path, what the police say the murderer used, to the clearing where his car was parked. He was carrying a spade. Dirty with earth it was. He'd been digging, no doubt of that."

It was a long speech, and appeared to exhaust the dying man. Again the doctor and the parson waited. Band smoothed his hand over his bald head. Payne loosened his clerical collar. They were both uncomfortably warm, and each seemed to expect the other to take charge of the conversation.

At last Payne said, "Where were you when you saw this, Mr. Finner? Presumably the man didn't see you."

"No. He didn't see me. I was having a widdle against a tree, and he was in a hell of a hurry to get to his car."

"Do you remember what day of the week this was?" Band asked.

The old man thought hard. "It wasn't Friday. That was the day her ladyship found the body. Nor the day before, because that was when I was taken sick again. Perhaps it was Tuesday or Wednesday?" he said hopefully.

"And you never told the police? That's what's been worrying you?" asked the parson. "Mr. Finner, there's no need to worry any more. You didn't realize what you'd seen until the body was found, and by then you were unfortunately a very sick man. God will understand."

"I don't go so much for God, but it's been on my conscience, like."

"Of course, but now you've told us you've nothing to worry about any more, Mr. Finner." The priest was not to be deterred. "God understands, as I said. He forgives all our sins, those of omission, those—"

The old man's eyes had closed. His hands fluttered on the coverlet and were still. The doctor rose, bent over him, felt his pulse and shook his head at Payne.

"Has he gone?"

"No. Not quite." He leaned nearer. "Tobias," he said urgently. "Tobias, who was it you saw in the wood?"

For a moment there was no answer. Payne and Band held their breaths. Then the eyes opened, and before they glazed, Tobias Finner said quite clearly, "Colonel Brevint. Colonel Jack Brevint. I recognized him plain."

Band and Payne stared at each other, before Band stooped over the bed and almost immediately drew the sheet up over Tobias Finner's face.

"He's gone at last," the doctor said. "I suppose the law would call that a dying declaration of a kind. We'll have to tell the police. Do you think we should make a note of his words before we forget them, and both sign it?"

"It won't do any harm," said Payne.

CHAPTER 8

"I think we ought to have a few people in for dinner this weekend," Lady Gerart announced at lunch the next day.

"Isn't this rather sudden?" Veronica yawned. She was bored. She would have gone up to London, but David was certain to be too busy at the House to pay her any attention. And all her friends seemed to be busy with interesting jobs; really, she would soon have to decide what she wanted to do.

"Nothing formal," said her mother. "But it's quite time we had Father Payne to a meal and—"

"With his glamorous sister."

"Of course, darling. And we're not sure she is so glamorous. I know that's what John Courtney said when we met him this morning in the Colombury Post Office, but I doubt if he's a good judge of glamour."

"Who else?"

"Well, Daddy and David will be here. That makes six with us." Constance Gerart considered. "And I thought we might ask the Brevints, and Simon Ashe and Sylvia. We do owe the Ashes."

"That sounds wildly exciting! And when's the great event to take place? Friday?"

"No. Saturday. Old Tobias Finner is being buried on Friday afternoon, and I shall have to go to the funeral," said Lady Gerart. "It would be nice if you came with me."

Veronica sighed. "All right. On one condition."

"Which is?"

"That I may run around this afternoon inviting all these lucky people to dinner on Saturday."

"Very well, though phone calls would be adequate. It's not a formal party, as I said."

"But it's eight for eight-thirty. And black tie," her daughter mocked her.

"Naturally," said Lady Gerart.

Veronica was fond of her mother, but life without David was dull. Roll on Friday, she thought, as she started the Mini, which had been her parents' eighteenth birthday present to her, and drove away from the Manor. She had decided to visit the Ashes first, and work her way round so that she could satisfy her curiosity by arriving at Church Cottage in time for tea with Father Payne and his sister. If they failed to ask her to tea, she would fall back on the Brevints in the old vicarage at the end of the lane.

She drove as fast as the Mini and the lanes would permit. The Ashes lived a couple of miles outside Fairfield on the far side of the village from the Manor. Their house was large and modern, but built of the traditional cream-coloured Cotswold stone. She parked behind the Rolls which stood before the massive front door, nodded to the uniformed chauffeur who sat at the wheel, and rang the bell.

The sight of the Mini and the Rolls standing side by side somehow pleased her. She didn't much like the Ashes, whom she regarded as snobs, nor their architect-designed, interior-decorated house. Further, she found Sylvia patronizing—after all, Veronica was no longer a schoolgirl. Simon was well aware of that; he didn't always keep his hands to himself, and she had had to slap him down once or twice.

She waited in the hall. Sylvia Ashe appeared almost at once. As always she was immaculately groomed and, since she was wearing a long mink coat over a tailored suit, it was obvious she was about to go out.

"Veronica dear! I'm just off to Oxford."

"That's all right." Veronica, who was envious of the mink

coat in spite of her determination never to wear real fur, yearned to address Sylvia as "dear" in return, but had never managed to summon up the courage.

"I won't take a moment. I'm merely a messenger," she said. "Mother invites you both to dinner on Saturday. She apologizes for the short notice, but it's a spur-of-the-moment party."

"How nice! Yes, I'm sure we'd love to come. I was looking at my little book minutes ago, and I know we're free. Informal, you said, Veronica? A family party?"

"Not exactly." Veronica widened her eyes at the very idea that the Ashes should be invited to a Gerarts' family party. "It's to welcome Father Payne, now that he's settled in, and his sister, now she's joined him. Eight for eight-thirty. Black tie."

"I see." Sylvia's smile was thin, as she appreciated the significance of Veronica's expression. She replied with full formality, "Please tell your mother that we accept with pleasure."

"And up yours!" Veronica said aloud as the chauffeured Rolls followed her Mini down the drive.

She was glad when it turned off and she could no longer see it in her rear-view mirror, but by the time she reached Church Cottage she had forgotten Sylvia Ashe. Her thoughts were on Blaise Payne. She was wondering why he hadn't mentioned after yesterday's Sunday morning service that he was expecting a relation to visit him the next day; it seemed an odd omission from the general conversation.

Kay opened the door, and looked inquiringly at Veronica, who thought that John Courtney hadn't exaggerated. Miss Payne, in black trousers and a yellow sweater, was certainly a glamorous character, with her red hair and her cigarette in a long holder. She smelt of smoke, unlike Sylvia Ashe who always wore the most expensive scents.

"Come in," she said at once when Veronica had introduced herself and explained her errand. "This is very kind of your mother. I'm sure we'd love to have dinner with you on Saturday, but I'd better ask Billy."

"Billy?"

"Oh dear! I've done it again." Kay laughed. "I'm afraid Blaise was always called Billy by the family when he was a child, and the name has stuck."

"Kay, who's there?"

Footsteps sounded on the stairs, and Father Payne appeared. Veronica got the impression that he was angry or agitated about something, and when she repeated the invitation there was a fractional hesitation before he accepted, saying they would be delighted. To her disappointment, however, they didn't ask her to stay to tea, although it was almost four o'clock.

She drove back along the lane past the Church of St. Blaise, and parked in front of the old vicarage. At least she could rely on Dorothy Brevint and the Colonel, she thought. With any luck there would be scones and homemade cake; Dorothy enjoyed cooking.

Mrs. Dolbel, who worked for the Brevints on Tuesdays and Thursdays, let her into the hall, but then seemed undecided about what she should do with her. Angry voices were coming from the drawing-room on the left. Unashamedly Veronica listened, but the door was almost shut and it was impossible to catch more than a few odd words.

"Disgraceful! Disgraceful, that's what it is! . . . the mumblings of a dying man . . . accuse me. I deny it, absolutely." That was Colonel Brevint. There were other voices too, Dorothy Brevint's, sounding tearful, and one that Veronica didn't recognize immediately. Then the drawing-room door was flung open, and the Colonel barked, "I'll ask you to leave my house, sir—and the young lady."

Mrs. Dolbel fled to the kitchen, but there was nowhere for Veronica to hide. She stood to one side as Colonel Brevint unceremoniously ushered Detective Chief Inspector Tansey and Sergeant Greenway past her. The Colonel was not tall, and he was overweight and always choleric-looking, but on this occasion he was purple in the face. He was normally a mild man, though it was obvious from his appearance that now he was extremely angry.

Veronica swallowed hard as the Colonel banged shut the front door and turned to face her. He stared at her, but as if he didn't recognize her, and it seemed an inappropriate moment to proffer an invitation to dinner. She was glad when Dorothy Brevint came into the hall.

Ignoring Veronica, the Colonel went straight to his wife, and put his arm around her shoulders. "It's all right, darling," he said. "Just a foolish foul-up. It'll get straightened out. You're not to worry."

"I'm quite all right, Jack." Dorothy Brevint smiled bravely. "Hello, Veronica dear. I didn't know you were here."

"Mrs.—Mrs. Dolbel let me in. I've just called to ask if you'll have dinner with us on Saturday." Veronica spoke hurriedly. She no longer wanted to stay to tea, but to leave as quickly as she could and escape from this extraordinary situation that she only partly understood. "Eight for eight-thirty. Black tie, as usual." She forgot to apologize for the short notice. "We do hope you can make it."

"Yes, I'm sure we can," Dorothy Brevint said. "Thank you very much."

"Good." Veronica moved towards the front door and the Colonel went to open it for her. "I'm so pleased. Till Saturday, then."

"We'll be there," said Colonel Brevint. "That is, unless that fool of a chief inspector has decided to arrest me."

No one in their senses would have called Dick Tansey a fool. "The man's a liar, and not a very good one," he said of Colonel Brevint as Sergeant Greenway drove their car away from Fairfield. "He was much too vehement in his denials, and in his contempt for old Tobias Finner. Too vehement altogether. At one point I thought he was going to have a coronary."

"Dying men are meant to tell the truth," remarked Greenway, "and Tobias had nothing to gain by maligning the Colonel. Even Brevint didn't suggest that the old man bore him a grudge; he could have used that as a ploy."

"Perhaps he wasn't quick enough to think of it." Tansey was

scornful. "He kept on about Finner muttering in his death throes and being misunderstood. But both Dr. Band, in whom I have great faith, and this new parson, Father Payne, were positive about what the old man said."

"So either Finner was mistaken or Brevint was lying?"

"Yes, and I'd settle for the latter. We'll let him stew overnight, and bring him in tomorrow morning—that's if the chief constable agrees. I think I'd better cover myself and consult him, because—" It was a minute before Tansey completed the sentence. "Because I don't believe Brevint's the killer. I'm not being psychic or anything, but I've got a kind of a hunch. In any case, I doubt if he's big or strong enough—especially with his heart condition—to have carried that body through the woods."

"But you think John Courtney could have managed it?"

"Yes. He's much the same age as Brevint and he's thin, but he's tall and wiry, and healthy. I'd say he had the strength," said Tansey. "But once more we're back to the same point—identification. At least we should soon know whether it's John Peter or not."

That morning Madge Ward, Peter Courtney's girlfriend, had come down from London in an attempt to identify the body found in Copley Wood. She had been composed, and far less shrill than she had sounded on the telephone. Tansey had been impressed, not least by her candour and honesty.

"I don't know," she had said. "I just do not know. You may think it odd, for after all we were living together and I saw him naked often enough, but I still don't know. I don't think that's Peter, but I couldn't swear to it either way. If—if only it had a face."

The body had no face, but it still possessed hands, and its fingerprints had been taken days ago. Tansey had no difficulty in persuading Miss Ward to allow expert officers from the Met to examine her flat, as soon as she returned to London. She admitted to not being "much of a housekeeper," and the chances that there would still be an abundance of Peter Courtney's prints around the place were excellent.

In fact, the Met had been most cooperative, and the results of their efforts were coming through on a facsimile link when Tansey and Greenway got back to headquarters. A quantity of fingerprints had been found in Miss Ward's flat. Most were hers but, excluding a few odd ones that probably belonged to workmen or friends, the rest were those of a man who, she said, could only be Peter Courtney. Neither they, nor any of the prints in the flat, corresponded with those of the unidentified corpse.

"So we can safely say that our unknown is not John Peter Courtney," said Chief Inspector Tansey.

"Which means we've no longer any reason to suspect his uncle," remarked Greenway.

Tansey was thoughtful. "It also means that we can accept the uncle's evidence that on the Friday afternoon, a week before Lady Gerart found the body, he was in that part of Copley Wood looking for his damned violets—and that he didn't see the silver button, or find any freshly turned earth. There's no doubt he's an intelligent, observant man, who was actually searching the ground, so we can assume that neither button nor new grave was there to be seen. And what conclusion can you draw from that, Sergeant?"

"The murder—or at any rate the burial—took place between John Courtney's visit to that bit of the wood on one Friday, and Lady Gerart's on the next."

"Yes, but more than that—it probably clears David Walden, in spite of his stupidity over the button. We know he drove down to Fairfield with Sir William on the Thursday of that week, and left with him again on the Monday morning, which would allow him only two possible days to do the job— and from the reports we've had they seem to have been pretty well occupied. Mind you, I'm not discarding him completely, but it's a pointer in his favour."

"So that leaves Colonel Brevint as the chief suspect, sir."

Tansey sighed. "I suppose so, at the moment, but I'm not happy about the situation. This damned case is never going to be solved until that body's identified."

CHAPTER 9

The rain started about ten o'clock that evening, and lasted throughout the night. It was still raining the next morning when Jane Mabson called at Church Cottage. Father Payne was up and dressed, and had eaten his breakfast. Mindful that Wednesday was one of Mrs. Dolbel's days, he had set the alarm early, and woken a reluctant Kay. When she had refused to leave the warmth of their bed, he had unceremoniously picked her up and dumped her on the bed in the guest room, where she was of course meant to be sleeping. Later, to placate her, he had taken her a cup of coffee and some toast, but she still had not come downstairs.

Miss Mabson, who had shed raincoat, umbrella and wellington boots in the hall and given them to Mrs. Dolbel, was greeted by Father Payne in the sitting-room. "A dreadful day, Miss Mabson. Surely you came by car?"

"I left it by the church. I've been looking at the plot where old Tobias Finner's to be buried on Friday, and I've called to discuss the details." Jane Mabson sat herself down in an upright chair, and looked with approval around the pleasant room which she and Constance Gerart had together created. Then she sniffed. "Do you smoke, Father?"

"No, Miss Mabson, I don't. But you know my sister's staying with me for a few days, and unfortunately she does. And some of my visitors—"

"If you don't smoke yourself, you shouldn't allow others to

smoke in here. It's your house, and the smoke gets in the curtains. The smell is horrible."

"Yes. I'm sorry if it worries you." With an effort Payne managed not to sound sarcastic. "You were talking about Mr. Finner's funeral, Miss Mabson."

"I was, indeed. Father, you know I've made myself responsible for the arrangements? He worked for me for years, and I feel I owe it to his family."

"That's very good of you, though from what he said I gather Mr. Finner was not a great churchgoer."

"That's as may be. But he has to be buried, and some of us in the country still like to conduct matters properly." Miss Mabson spoke with satisfaction. "The gravediggers will be here tomorrow morning, but they shouldn't worry you. Cresford will look after them. One good thing about this rain is that it will make the ground easier to dig."

"But let us hope it doesn't rain on Friday. Rain at a funeral is terribly sad."

"Do you think so, Father?" said Miss Mabson. "Strangely enough, I'm not sure I agree with you. However—the undertakers will be bringing the coffin to the church on Thursday afternoon. I hope that will be convenient for you."

"Yes, of course, Miss Mabson," said Payne, and thought that it would have made very little difference if he had been prepared to claim that it was extremely inconvenient.

Miss Mabson went on, "Finner was a great gardener, as you know, but there'll be only family flowers. That was Finner's request, though I shall certainly send a wreath myself, of course. The casket—it's just a plain pine affair. Better to give his daughter some money than bury it with him. It'll be covered by a pall. Cresford will organize matters." She paused. "Now, to choose the hymns and the form of service. His daughter has left everything to me."

"Yes," said the parson, who could well understand how this had come about, and made a mental resolution to be equally amenable.

They were interrupted by Mrs. Dolbel, bringing them morning coffee and biscuits. There were three cups on the tray. Immediately afterwards slow, languid steps on the stairs stopped Miss Mabson in mid-sentence, and the smell of cigarette smoke preceded Kay into the sitting-room. Miss Mabson stared.

"Hello," said Kay. "Coffee. Good. Pour me a cup, will you, Billy dear. Hot and black."

"Good morning." Jane Mabson recovered her manners. She had been hoping to meet the priest's sister, but she hadn't expected this extraordinary creature in a flimsy nightgown, which she made only a minimal effort to draw across her body. It did nothing to hide her figure. Admittedly she was small and slight, but she had full breasts, and one couldn't help but notice the reddish triangle at her crotch. "You must be Miss Payne," Jane Mabson said, looking away hurriedly.

"Yes—I'm Kay." She drew on her cigarette and blew a cloud of smoke into the air.

"I—I'm sorry. I should have introduced you." The Reverend Blaise Payne at last found his voice. "Miss Mabson, as you know, this is my sister, Kay Payne."

Jane Mabson nodded acknowledgement, and did her best to smile. She was sorry for Father Payne, but the woman would have to leave, and very soon; she was impossible—an obvious slut, still not dressed at ten in the morning, but with her face already made up. There was no way the Parochial Church Council could permit such a creature to remain for any length of time at Church Cottage with her brother. Miss Mabson was glad to see from his expression that the priest seemed to share her opinion.

As he passed Kay a cup of coffee Payne's hand shook, and when he spoke his voice was harsh. "Kay, Miss Mabson and I are discussing arrangements for a funeral on Friday. Would you mind taking your coffee into another room?"

Kay hesitated. "No, I don't mind," she said, "providing it's not my funeral you're arranging, Billy dear. Goodbye, Miss Mabson. Nice to have met you."

And, blowing another cloud of cigarette smoke in their direction, Kay went. Miss Mabson fanned herself and coughed. She managed to murmur goodbye, but Kay had closed the door behind her. And Miss Mabson decided to say nothing to Father Payne about his preposterous sister for the moment, not until she had consulted Constance Gerart.

"To return to Tobias Finner," she said. "I thought I might say a few words. Not a eulogy, of course. He scarcely warrants that, but something simple—" She broke off. "Father, are you listening?"

"Yes, yes, Miss Mabson," Payne assured her. "I was just thinking about—poor old Tobias."

As the police car which was conveying him to the headquarters of the Thames Valley Police and an unpleasant interview with Chief Inspector Tansey sped towards Kidlington, Colonel Jack Brevint was also thinking of Tobias Finner. His thoughts were not charitable. Indeed, he was wishing the dead man all the miseries of hell. It made no difference to the Colonel that his present predicament was due to his own stupidity and no fault of Finner's.

He had been awake half the night, forced to lie still so as not to disturb Dorothy, who snored gently in the double bed beside him. But he still hadn't made up his mind. If he told the truth, she would know he had lied to her, and Dorothy set great store by not telling even minor fibs. If he didn't, he might land in jail, which was absurd because he hadn't killed the wretched man, whoever he was. If only old Tobias hadn't seen him with the spade . . .

By the time they reached Kidlington, and Colonel Brevint had spent twenty minutes in a bare interrogation room with a uniformed constable standing by the door, he was so nervous he felt sick. This was a new experience for him. He had been a brave soldier, and one prepared to take decisions, but he remained at a loss as to his best course of action.

Chief Inspector Tansey came into the room, and motioned to the constable to leave them. As the door closed he sat down opposite Colonel Brevint and laid a file on the table between them. "Now, Colonel," he said, "we're quite alone. No microphones, no nothing. So will you please tell me why you've chosen to waste my time like this?"

"I—I don't know what you mean." The Colonel fell back on aggressiveness, but it didn't deceive Tansey, who had also been reconsidering the case overnight.

"Sir," he said, almost pleadingly, "I know perfectly well you didn't kill that man buried in Copley Wood, not unless someone helped you to carry him to where he was found, but I must have an explanation for Tobias Finner's dying statement."

"I never said I did—kill anyone, I mean. I told you the old man Finner didn't know what he was saying. He was round the bend. It was an absurd accusation. He was probably thinking of something or someone quite different. He—"

"No!" Tansey interrupted brutally. "Dr. Band assures me that Mr. Finner was perfectly clear-headed and knew exactly what he was saying. He had made a point of asking the priest —the Reverend Blaise Payne—to be there, with the doctor. Finner's daughter says he seemed to think of it as a kind of deathbed confession. He was worried because he hadn't told anyone before."

"All right! But he could have been mistaken," Brevint said. "He might have believed it was me when it was someone else."

Tansey stared at Brevint in disgust. He said nothing. The Colonel fidgeted in his chair; he knew that his last comment had been ludicrous. He was not someone easily mistaken, and Tobias—who had occasionally done odd jobs at the old vicarage—was no stranger to him.

"Very well, Chief Inspector." Jack Brevint threw in his hand. "I'm sorry—and I mean that. I *was* in Copley Wood. I *was* carrying a spade. It *was* the Wednesday before Lady Gerart found the body. The only thing Finner got wrong was that I hadn't been burying a man. I'd been burying my wife's dog."

Tansey showed no surprise. "What sort of dog?" he asked mildly. "And how exactly did you bury it?"

If the Colonel thought the chief inspector's reaction odd, he didn't comment. "It was a wire-haired terrier bitch," he said. "Spayed. Her name was Minnie. My wife was devoted to her. She went missing a day or two before, and eventually, quite by chance, I found her in a hedge on the road near our house. She must have been killed by a car. She was a dreadful sight, poor little thing. I couldn't let Dorothy see her like that, so I put her in a box, an old carton I had, and buried her in the woods. My wife still expects her to be found somewhere, to come back to her, and I—I've had to pretend I do too," he concluded miserably.

The chief inspector nodded. "But once Mr. Finner had made his statement concerning you, Colonel, why didn't you tell us about the dog at once, instead of persisting in your denial that the old man had seen you?"

"Because of my wife, Chief Inspector." The Colonel sighed. "She would feel I'd deceived her and—and she'd take it badly."

"Ah!" Tansey wondered if the chief constable—or, for that matter, the Commissioner of the Metropolitan Police—ever really understood people and their curious motives any better than he did.

"All right, Colonel," he said at length. "I won't lecture you any more about wasting police time. As far as we're concerned that's the end of the matter, except—we did find your Minnie, you know. She was dug up when the wood was being searched, in a carton as you said, and at the moment she's in cold storage. Do you want us to dispose of her?"

"Yes, please! You'll—cremate her?"

"Well, yes. Or we'll get the local RSPCA to do it for us. We're not really in the business of cremating bodies, you know—animal or human. I suggest you tell your wife the full story, Colonel." Tansey hadn't the least idea what would happen to the dead dog, but he had no qualms about quieting the Colonel's concern.

"Thank you, Chief Inspector. Thank you very much." The

Colonel reached across the desk, and offered Tansey his hand. Tansey took it. "I'm most grateful."

Tansey said, "That's all right, Colonel Brevint. Next time, tell the police everything, and as soon as possible. I'll get a car to take you home."

Ten minutes later the chief inspector was in his office, re-counting the details of the interview to Sergeant Greenway. "At least that's solved one problem," he said.

"And I've got the solution to another, sir," said Greenway. "Mr. Courtney telephoned earlier. He's had a postcard from his nephew, John Peter, saying he had departed to darkest Devon to write a book. Anyway, I had the local police check, and John Peter Courtney's alive and well in the Southwest."

Tansey shook his head in mock despair. "So that leaves us—after a considerable amount of work and effort, and the ex-penditure of a good deal of the taxpayers' money—with an unidentified corpse and not a single suspect. It's precisely where we came in."

"Cheer up, sir," said Greenway. "It seems ages since the body was found, but in fact it will only be a week on Friday."

As so often happened, Tansey thought, a bout of feverish ac-tivity at the commencement of an investigation was being followed by a lull, all the initial leads having come to nothing. As far as the present case was concerned, there were admit-tedly two or three members of the Nectar and Ambrosia Club who hadn't yet been traced, but there was little hope that any of them would prove relevant. It was now Friday, and the dead man remained unidentified.

On an impulse Tansey decided to attend Tobias Finner's fu-neral. At least it would be an excuse to have another look at Fairfield, and some of the people who seemed to be involved in the affair. Then he would complete his report to the chief constable, admit he was baffled and at a dead end, and ask for instructions.

Sergeant Greenway was busy, so Tansey drove himself. He arrived at St. Blaise's Church late, and the service had already begun. Heads turned as the great door swung shut behind him, and he found himself conspicuous. He had forgotten the size of the church, and the likely small number of people in the congregation.

There were in fact about twenty, all clustered in the front pews. If he did not want to emphasize his presence he had to join them, though he chose a pew by himself. Veronica Gerart gave him a wide smile as he sat down, but he did not respond.

The service was short. Miss Mabson spoke for five minutes on the virtues of Tobias Finner's long life. Someone unknown to Tansey read a lesson in a thick Oxfordshire accent. The Reverend Blaise Payne said some simple prayers, and there was a last hymn.

Tansey would have slipped away as the coffin was carried on the shoulders of the Colombury undertaker's pall-bearers, but he decided to try the side door, and unfortunately the coffin, the pall-bearers, the parson and the members of Tobias Finner's family who were to attend the interment had arranged to use the same exit, and reached it at the same time as the chief inspector. Tansey therefore witnessed a small but interesting incident.

There was a shallow, wide step outside this church door. It was unexpected, and took one of the pall-bearers by surprise. He staggered. The coffin lurched dangerously and, if it had not been for Payne's quick action in supporting it, would have fallen to the ground.

"Christ!" said Payne. Then he swallowed hard. "Christ— have mercy," he corrected himself quickly.

Standing so close that he could see the sheen of sweat on Payne's upper lip, Chief Inspector Tansey knew that the correction—the addition—had been an afterthought.

CHAPTER 10

"Jane, I've a great favour to ask of you," said Lady Gerart on the telephone. "I'm giving a most boring dinner party tonight. It was meant to be for Father Blaise and his sister. Rather impromptu. My conscience pricked me. And now—"

"The answer is no, Constance," Miss Mabson interrupted firmly. "That is, if you're asking me to fill in an unexpected gap for you. I have, as you are aware, met Miss Payne once. I have no wish to meet her again. She struck me as a most undesirable dinner guest. Apart from anything else, she would certainly smoke between courses. So, thank you, but no. Any other time, if I'm free, I should be happy to come, but not tonight."

"Jane, I *was* going to ask you to dinner, but not with Miss Payne. It is she who's deserted us. Probably a good thing in the circumstances, as you suggest," Constance Gerart said frankly. "Father Payne telephoned to say she'd unexpectedly decided to return to London, and he was driving her into Oxford to catch a train."

"Good! Excellent news! I hope she won't be returning."

"I gathered not—at least not in the near future." Lady Gerart laughed. "You don't sound very charitable, Jane, but I gather you'll come this evening. Eight o'clock?"

"I don't feel particularly charitable about that girl, Constance," said Miss Mabson curtly, "even if she did have a nervous breakdown. She probably brought it on herself. Anyway,

I think she's a definite minus as our priest's sister here. But I accept your invitation with pleasure. Very many thanks."

The guests were assembled in the Gerarts' drawing-room. The houseman was serving pre-dinner drinks amid talk and laughter and general conviviality. Lady Gerart was a practised hostess, and tonight was a simple, if dull, party; everyone knew everyone and there was little for her to do. The food would be good—she was lucky that her housekeeper enjoyed cooking—and the wines would be excellent; Sir William always insisted on choosing them himself.

Inevitably the conversation turned to the Feast of St. Blaise, which was now so close. All the arrangements had been made —the early Communion, the sung matins, the parish lunch in the crypt afterwards and the speeches—but a lot of work remained, and could only be done immediately before the celebration.

"—extremely fortunate the feast falls on a Sunday this year."

"Yes, many more people should come. We ought to have a much larger congregation than usual."

"We've already had a surprising number of acceptances, or at least indications that people will be there—for the food, if nothing else."

"Do we mind if they don't come to the service first?"

"I really don't know what the policy is. It's a nice point—"

"The silver will need a final polish before it goes over to the church."

"The evening before? Yes, we want to get it over there, so that Father Payne can arrange it first thing on the Sunday morning."

"—safe? Oh yes, it'll be perfectly safe. We have a special place to put it away, and anyway no one will know it's there. Most people are unaware that the really valuable stuff usually stays right in this house. They'll see no reason why the arrangements should be any different."

"—spring flowers in Colombury. I assume they've come

from the Scillies or the Channel Islands. Of course, they're awfully expensive, but this is a special occasion—"

"—a very special occasion indeed. A double celebration. For the Feast Day of St. Blaise, and for Father Blaise himself—our own priest at last."

It was Constance Gerart who made the last remark, and as she stopped speaking a small silence fell. Everyone was suddenly conscious that Father Payne, who might be considered the guest of honour that evening, had not yet arrived. In the silence the large antique long-case clock in the corner of the room chimed the half-hour, and it was accepted that dinner would be announced in a few minutes. But Payne was not there.

"Where is the darned fellow?" said Sir William. "He's late. That clock's never wrong."

"He must have been delayed," Lady Gerart intervened quickly. "I'm sure he'll be here soon."

She crossed the room to tell the houseman that dinner should be postponed for a few minutes, and her guests politely resumed their conversations. But the atmosphere was no longer so relaxed. Everyone was waiting doubtfully, wondering what might have happened. It was a great relief when the doorbell sounded and, moments later, Father Payne was shown into the room.

"Lady Gerart, I'm so sorry. I do apologize," he said. "I had to take my sister into Oxford, as I told you, and I had trouble with my car on the way back."

"Well, you're here now, Father. We were beginning to worry." Automatically Father Payne had held out his hand, and Lady Gerart had made to take it. She stopped suddenly. "You've hurt your hand again," she said.

Payne looked at his bandaged hand as if in surprise. "I—I knocked it," he said, "and the cut re-opened so I had to go back to a bandage. Sticking plaster wasn't adequate."

Lady Gerart made sympathetic noises, and Sir William said, "I hope you can hold a glass, Payne. There's just time for a quick drink before we have dinner."

Payne thanked him and asked for a glass of white wine, which was produced at once. He drank it quickly, and almost at once they went into the dining-room. He found himself seated on Lady Gerart's right with Jane Mabson on his other side, and Colonel Brevint and Veronica opposite them. The other end of the table had Sir William at its head, with the Ashes, Dorothy Brevint and David Walden.

Lady Gerart gestured to Father Payne, and after a minimal hesitation all rose to their feet while the priest said a brief grace. Dinner then passed pleasantly, and the table was small enough for conversation to be fairly general. Veronica, for instance, showed some curiosity about Kay, but Payne found her questions easy to parry. Otherwise his only problem was his bandaged right hand. It wasn't until the ladies had retired, and the port was circulating, that there was any acrimony.

Sir William said something about the police not making much headway with the Copley Wood case, and Colonel Brevint, who by now had drunk a fair amount, couldn't resist the temptation. He gave a deep, raucous laugh. Immediately the others stared at him, while he stared at Father Payne.

"Ask Mr. Payne to explain," he said. "Ask him how he's been persuading Chief Inspector Tansey to occupy his time with old Tobias Finner's mutterings. Talk about wasting police effort and public money!"

Payne's sallow skin flushed with anger. "I'm glad for your sake, Colonel Brevint, that you were able to satisfy the chief inspector," he said coldly. "But may I point out that it was Dr. Band and not I who contacted the police, though naturally I supported him. In the circumstances, we had no alternative. It was our duty."

"What on earth are you talking about?" Sir William intervened. "You've not been accusing the Colonel here of anything to do with that body, have you, Payne?"

"As good as," said Brevint sourly.

"Mr. Finner made what might be called a deathbed confession or a dying declaration to Dr. Band and myself," Payne explained. "We decided that we had to tell the police."

"But where does Jack come in?" asked Simon Ashe.

The Colonel answered for himself. "Dorothy's dog had been killed. I didn't want her to know, or to see the poor brute's mangled body, so I buried it myself in Copley Wood. Evidently Finner saw me there with a spade, and jumped to the wrong conclusion. The old fool!"

Everyone but the priest laughed, and even the Colonel was forced to grin. The parts played by Band and Payne still annoyed him, but perhaps there was an amusing aspect of the affair. And certainly, when he had taken the chief inspector's advice and told Dorothy the truth, she had taken it well.

David Walden said, "I suppose it wasn't you who killed Mrs. Brevint's dog, Father Payne?"

"Of course not!" The priest was emphatic.

"Actually, it was a cat you hit on your way down here, wasn't it?" Sir William said as he recirculated the port. "Have you heard any more about the incident?"

"No, Sir William." Payne's hand shook a little as he refilled his glass. "I don't expect to, either. The accident happened some way north of here."

"That reminds me," said Simon Ashe suddenly. "I met a chap in the City last week. He came from the North originally, but he claimed to have known you in London, Father Payne." Ashe grinned as if he found this amusing. "A chap called Gordon Crane, the barrister. He said you'd be sure to remember him. He was prosecuting some attractive girl, and you were the chief witness of the defence. He said your evidence got her off though she was guilty as hell."

"Gordon Crane? Really?" said Payne.

"Yes. Incidentally, he's invited himself to spend a weekend with Sylvia and me. He hopes to renew his acquaintance with you."

"When is this to be?" Payne asked quickly.

Ashe shrugged. "He's coming sometime after the end of the month."

Sir William stared doubtfully from Ashe to Payne; there were undercurrents here he failed to understand. He pushed back his chair and rose to his feet before any further conversation could take place.

"I think we'd better join the ladies," he said.

The dinner party broke up early, to the relief of Lady Gerart, who felt that it had not been one of her better evenings. Miss Mabson, pleading a headache, was the first to leave, and Father Payne, who had been yearning to go as soon as possible, seized the opportunity to follow her.

He drove slowly back to Church Cottage. It had been one hell of a day, he thought. Every damned thing seemed to have gone wrong. After all Kay's things were packed, Mrs. Dolbel had "popped in" with some laundry she had done for her, and while she was fussing around, he had burnt his breakfast toast. That was trivial in comparison with what had happened later.

In the first place, his old car had refused to start. He had been struggling with that when a girl had roared up on a moped and demanded to know why he hadn't been at home the previous evening, when she and her fiancé had made arrangements to discuss their wedding, which was set for the end of March. He had been forced to apologize, saying that the appointment had completely slipped his memory. But he knew the bad mark he had earned would soon be public knowledge throughout the parish.

It had been a relief to reach Oxford. Once there, he had managed to complete his errands satisfactorily, though the trip had not been trouble-free. He had met his rural dean, who had kept him talking on a cold, windy street. Immediately after that, he had literally bumped into John Courtney.

"Well, Father Payne! What a surprise!" Courtney had said. "We're always meeting in Oxford, it seems. But you're alone today. What have you done with your charming sister?"

"I'm afraid she's had to go back to London."

"Really? I hadn't heard."

Payne had done his best to be affable. "When she visits me again I hope you'll come and have supper with us."

"Oh, you mustn't bother with an old man like me," Court- ney had said. "You've more important fish to fry. You're dining at the Manor tonight, or so our mutual friend Mrs. Dolbel tells me. You can't keep a secret for long in Fairfield, you know, Father Payne."

"An invitation to dinner is hardly a secret, Mr. Courtney," Payne had said.

"I hope you enjoy your dinner," Courtney had said at length. "At least you'll get plenty of good food."

But of course he had not enjoyed the dinner, Payne thought bitterly. There had been that idiot Brevint crowing at his own cleverness in proving the police and the doctor—and the par- son—fools to accept old Tobias Finner's accusation, when it was so obviously ludicrous. Then Ashe had produced Gordon Crane, with his old story.

"My past catching up with me," Payne said to himself re- signedly, and suddenly, as the irony of the situation hit him, he gave a short laugh.

As they were going to bed, Sir William recounted to his wife the exchanges after dinner between Simon Ashe and Father Payne. "Ashe seemed to think it was funny," he said, "and Payne got all uptight. Ashe told me afterwards that the girl was a known prostitute, though on this occasion she'd been accused of theft. Apparently, the barrister chap had suspected that Payne had lied to save her, though he admitted he could have been wrong. Anyway, it's perturbing, isn't it?"

"I shouldn't worry, darling," said Lady Gerart, at the dress- ing-table removing her jewellery. "Theo Payne gave his nephew what amounted to a reference in recommending him to us."

"I know, dear. I may be tilting at windmills, but there's enough scandal in the church without St. Blaise adding to it. And remember, Constance, I'm the patron. It would rub off on me. I know we won't get another parson, but I'll really have to look into Payne's record."

"Yes dear, but—"

"But what?" Sir William demanded, on his way to the bathroom to clean his teeth.

"Of course, you're right, darling," said Constance Gerart, "but please, leave it till after the feast. Once that's over you can make all the inquiries you like. Indeed, it would only be reasonable before starting to consider confirming Payne in the living. Remember, at the moment he's merely the priest-in-charge, and has no formal status."

Sir William got slowly into his bed. "All right," he said, "I could leave it till after your feast. A week shouldn't make any difference."

CHAPTER 11

The week that followed was busy for all those connected with
the Church of St. Blaise—and for some who were not directly
interested. The great feast was to take place, of course, on
Sunday, February 3, when the obscure martyred bishop was
to be duly celebrated in the church so oddly dedicated to him.
This meant that the arrangements for the celebrations and
functions had to be ready by Saturday evening at the latest,
and Lady Gerart, as chairman of the committee in charge, was
determined to do everything possible to ensure that everything *should* be ready.

She herself was prepared to work hard, and she expected
her colleagues to do the same. The church was being given a
yet more thorough cleaning than usual, the woodwork was
dusted meticulously, the brass and the floor were polished and
polished again. The result was that by Saturday afternoon everything gleamed, and there was a pleasant smell of furniture
polish throughout the building. Then began the task of flower
arrangement.

Meanwhile, a succession of choir practices had been held,
and it had been discovered that Sylvia Ashe had a light, but
trained voice, the existence of which she had kept a secret
until now. "Principal boy in pantomimes when she was
younger, if you ask me," John Courtney had remarked to Father Payne acidly.

In reply Father Payne had managed a vague smile. There

was only one word to describe his feelings—fraught. He could readily remember festivities in his father's church when he was a boy, at Christmas and Easter and Harvest Thanksgiving, but his father had never seemed to be overwhelmed by the demands made on him. Here, before the Feast of St. Blaise, he himself seemed to be under the most constant pressure.

He was consulted about every single detail, even though his knowledge of local affairs—or even the affairs of the saint himself—was clearly limited. Hymns, lessons, the length of the service, the number of candles, the organ voluntaries, the silver to be displayed on the altar, what trousers or skirts the choir should wear under their surplices, whether or not daffodils should be mixed with the tulips and irises or displayed in separate arrangements, how the food for the buffet lunch after matins should be arranged on the trestle tables in the crypt— no one, not even Lady Gerart, seemed to be able to take a final decision without consulting him.

It was true, he reflected, that some of them, especially Lady Gerart, had already made up their minds and decided what should be done, but his confirmation that their decisions were in accord with his wishes was required. The situation was ludicrous.

He had done his best to minimize most of the consultations —certainly those less directly concerned with the services themselves. "Do whatever you consider best, ladies. I'm sure you know better than I do," he had found himself constantly repeating. But his litany had no effect. The responses were always identical: "But we want your opinion, Father. Tell us what you think."

The result was that, except for those hours of the night when he might reasonably have been expected to be asleep in bed, Father Payne had no time to himself—no time at which he might not be interrupted. His temper was becoming frayed.

He was not alone in feeling the strain. On Saturday afternoon Sylvia Ashe went so far as to swear at Miss Mabson, who had inadvertently knocked over a vase, drenching Sylvia's cashmere skirt with dirty water. Dorothy Brevint burst into tears when John Courtney told her that she was tone deaf, and had no place in any choir with claims to rudimentary competence. It took all Lady Gerart's tact to restore a temporary peace, but even she was beginning to feel the pace.

"Perhaps it's fortunate that the Feast of St. Blaise only comes once a year," she remarked tritely to Payne. "I must say I didn't realize how much work it was going to mean—even though the caterers are looking after the food."

"I hope you'll consider yourself amply rewarded tomorrow, Lady Gerart, when it all turns out to be a great success. There's every indication that the whole thing will be a memorable . . ."

Payne's voice trailed away. Constance Gerart turned to him, and saw that his mouth was slightly open, and his pallid face had taken on a greenish tinge. His breathing was fast and shallow.

"Father, what is it?" she asked at once. "Are you unwell?"

When he failed to answer she followed his gaze, which seemed to be fixed on the back of the church. In spite of the notice posted outside that St. Blaise was closed to visitors for the day, two people, whom she had never seen before, had entered the building. They were short-haired, much the same height and wearing jeans under padded anoraks, so that at first she thought they were both men. Then, as they began to walk down the aisle, she realized that the one with fair hair was a girl.

They had already been spotted by other workers or members of the committee, but it was Miss Mabson who approached them. The sense of her words was obvious, and they made no demur. With apologetic smiles and a last lingering look around, they turned and left the church. By now Payne had regained control of himself.

"I'm so sorry, Lady Gerart," he said. "Did I frighten you?"

"No, not exactly." She hesitated. "Father, did you recognize that couple who just came into the church?"

"No. I'm afraid I scarcely noticed them. I was too busy

thinking about myself. I do apologize, Lady Gerart, but I had a sudden sharp pain in my chest."

She regarded him anxiously, appalled by the thought that the priest was about to be taken ill at this crucial time. "Have you had it before?" she asked.

"Once or twice, when I've been overdoing things a bit." Payne smiled ruefully.

Lady Gerart did not return the smile. She decided that before there was any question of confirming Father Payne's appointment they would have to be reassured that he was in good health; they didn't want a sick priest at St. Blaise. "Perhaps you should go and rest for a while, Father," she said.

"No!" Payne spoke so sharply that he had to apologize yet again. "I'm sorry, Lady Gerart, but I—I couldn't rest at the moment. There's still quite a lot to be done. I know I could leave it to your excellent supervision, but I'm sure you appreciate that in the end it's my responsibility. I'll go to bed early tonight, and I'll be fine in the morning." Aware that he was talking too much, Payne stopped.

These views were such a sudden change from his earlier and obvious attempts to avoid or at least delegate responsibility that Lady Gerart stared at the priest in surprise. However, biting her tongue, she temporized.

"Very well. As you wish, Father. But I do think you should see Dr. Band about those chest pains." She nodded towards two approaching figures, carrying obviously heavy bags.

"Ah, here are my husband and David Walden," she said, glad to be able to change the subject. "They'll have brought over the silver we're going to use tomorrow. The altar should look magnificent with those Georgian candlesticks."

Thinking that the priest seemed to have infected her with his own odd nervousness, Lady Gerart, followed by Payne, went to meet the couple. They had taken their bags into the Lady Chapel, and Tom Cresford, the verger, had materialized from nowhere.

"Shall I open it for you, Sir William?" he asked.

Sir William Gerart took his time about answering. For a full minute he peered through the intricate stone masonry into the main body of the church. Then, having made sure that no one was taking any undue interest in their activities, he turned back.

"Yes. All right, Cresford," he said, motioning to Walden to leave his bag and stand at the entrance to the chapel to stop any unwelcome intruders.

While the others watched, the verger bent down and pushed at the stone near the floor, which caused part of the wall to swing open and reveal the large aperture. Hurriedly Sir William thrust the two bags of silver into the hidey-hole, and Cresford immediately shut the concealed door.

"Good," said Lady Gerart. "The silver will be quite safe there till tomorrow morning."

"Personally, I'm sure it will," Sir William agreed. "But I was talking to our insurance broker in London and he maintains that if by any unlikely chance it were to be stolen from this place, his firm would be justified in not paying up. Some rubbish about required precautions not being taken."

"That's absurd. It's spent the night there before, and they've never objected—"

"They didn't know," remarked Sir William drily.

"Anyway," Lady Gerart protested, "it's as safe in the hidey-hole as at the Manor. After all, we've been burgled there, and we could be again, and it's vastly more convenient to have it here overnight. Then Father Payne and Cresford can get it out in plenty of time for the early service. Don't you agree, Father?"

"If that was what was done when it was used on previous occasions, Lady Gerart, I see no objection," Payne said carefully, "but of course if Sir William thinks it might be better . . ."

"I admit that it'll be much more convenient to have it on the spot, and I've been wondering if we might ask Cresford to spend the night here, on guard," Sir William said tentatively. "That would solve the problem." He turned to the verger. "We're intending to leave the central heating on ready for tomorrow, so it won't be cold, and we can make you moderately comfortable. What do you say, Cresford?"

The verger's answer was surprisingly unequivocal. In no circumstances would he spend the night alone in the church. He wasn't a superstitious man, but however snug he might be able to make himself, he wouldn't get a wink of sleep—not a wink. And anyway Mrs. Cresford would never allow it. She expected him to be in bed beside her as a good husband should.

Veronica, who by now had joined the group, snorted with laughter at this point, and received a reproachful glance from her mother. But Cresford had made his position plain, and Sir William was forced to accept his decision. The silver would remain unguarded in its secret hidey-hole overnight, as it had done on other occasions.

"There's no reason why tonight should be any different," Lady Gerart repeated decisively. "It'll be quite safe, so don't let any of us worry."

After dinner at the Manor Lady Gerart suggested a rubber of bridge, but Sir William said he had papers to study, so they would have to play three-handed. David Walden, who hated all card games, wondered what excuse he could make, since clearly Sir William had no need of his services. He was about to open his mouth when Veronica provided him with an excuse.

"I was hoping David might come to St. Blaise with me," she said. "Rather like Tom Cresford, I'm not too keen on being there alone after dark."

"But why go over there at all, for heaven's sake, Veronica? You've been there most of the day," Lady Gerart expostulated.

"I've lost my gold bracelet. I know I dropped it in the church, and I think I know where." Veronica gave an innocent smile as her mother regarded her doubtfully. "I remember hearing a sort of tinkle when I was up in the organ loft."

"Can't you leave it till tomorrow?"

"I'd rather not. I'm very fond of that bracelet, and I'd hate to lose it." Veronica gave Walden a demure glance. "You won't mind coming with me, will you, David?"

"No-o. No, not at all," said Walden.

"Good. We'll take my Mini. With any luck I'll find the bracelet exactly where I'm pretty sure I dropped it, and we'll be back in no time."

"Very well." Lady Gerart wasn't prepared to make an issue of it. If there was no hope of bridge, she would take a book to bed with her and have an early night. "I'll fetch the key of the side door of the church for you."

"I think it was the mention of the Mini that did the trick," Veronica said as David drove away from the Manor. "Mother just couldn't visualize us intertwined on the back seat. Much too uncomfortable."

"She's quite right, too. I've no intention of trying. I don't want to dislocate my spine."

Veronica laughed. "You're the most unromantic man I ever met," she said. She opened her bag, produced her gold bracelet and put it on. "There we are. Found!"

"And you're one of the most devious women I ever met," retorted David. "What do I do now? Turn the Mini round and go back to the Manor?"

"Certainly not! I should never forgive you." She snuggled up to him. "David, we've not made love for weeks, and here's our chance. The church's central heating's being left on. The organ loft will be reasonably warm, and I've put some old pillows and a blanket in the back of the Mini. What do you say?"

"That you're incredible."

"It would solve all our problems if we got married."

"My darling Veronica, what it would most certainly do is make our sex life simpler. That's all. Other things wouldn't be so easy. In the first place I suspect your father would kick me out on my ear at the mere suggestion of our marriage. He knows as well as you do that I've no money and few prospects, and you're his beloved only child."

"Hm-m, we shall have to see."

"For heaven's sake! I can't afford to lose my job, Veronica, and I'm very much afraid your mother already suspects your intentions, if not mine."

"She likes you."

"Sure, maybe. But that doesn't necessarily mean she wants me as a son-in-law."

"All right." Veronica paused. "Look, here we are at the church. If you'd like to drop me off I can go and ask Father Payne to help me search for my bracelet. I expect he'd be happy to oblige, and drive me home afterwards."

David could have slapped her. "That's an absurd suggestion, Veronica, as you know perfectly well," he said. "So don't be an idiot, darling. Where are these damned pillows?"

It was indeed an absurd suggestion, though neither David nor Veronica could possibly have been aware of the reason.

At that moment the Reverend Blaise Payne was feeling desperate. He was sitting in his kitchen, his head buried in his hands, and he was literally grinding his teeth. Occasionally he swore aloud. He was hungry, having had no more than a sandwich at noon, but he couldn't bring himself to eat.

He waited. There seemed no alternative. He had thought of packing a suitcase and clearing out, but where could he go at such short notice that would be safe? He had very little cash and he didn't even have a decent car that would make a quick sale. Fleetingly the idea of taking the Georgian candlesticks from their resting-place in the Lady Chapel crossed his mind, only to be dismissed; they would be traced too easily.

In any event, the Reverend Blaise Payne couldn't just disappear on the eve of the blessed—or blasted—Feast Day. There would be an instant hue and cry. The police would be called, and his difficulties would be compounded. No, he had only one option. He must wait, and when his erstwhile friends arrived—and he doubted if they'd waste much time—he'd have to try to bluff his way out.

He cursed Kay. He had been a fool not to realize that, though she was still perfectly happy to go to bed with him, she wouldn't hesitate to sick the others on to him. It had come as a frightening shock to see the two of them walking up the church aisle that afternoon, towards himself and Lady Gerart.

At last he raised his head, certain that he had heard a car. Squaring his shoulders, he walked firmly into the hall as the doorbell rang. He was thankful that the waiting was over.

CHAPTER 12

David Walden woke slowly and sensuously. Then he became aware of his intense discomfort. The bed was hard. The bed? He opened his eyes. It was dark. He could see nothing, but he was conscious of lying on the floor in a narrow space, his legs entwined with what seemed to be wooden uprights—the supports of a bench, perhaps—and his back pressed firmly against what he realized was Veronica's soft and half-naked body. As he stirred, she gave a gentle snore.

Stifling his laughter now that he had oriented himself, David looked at the luminous dial of his watch. He gasped, and groped for the torch that Veronica had so thoughtfully brought with them to add verisimilitude to the search for her supposedly lost bracelet. He found the torch and switched it on. His first impression had not been wrong. The time was ten minutes to twelve.

His desire to laugh quenched instantly, David sat up and shook Veronica. "Come on, darling! Wake up!" He had an unpleasant vision of Lady Gerart telling her husband that her daughter had had an accident or been kidnapped, and the police must be called immediately. "It's almost midnight," he said.

"Oh, is that all?" Veronica yawned. She shivered and pulled the blanket over her body. "You sounded so agitated, darling, I thought it must be morning. I expected to see the choir in their stalls and Father Payne in his full regalia and the congregation all wearing the new hats they've bought to celebrate St. Blaise's Day. It's as dark as hell," she added.

"Not really," said David, whose eyes had by this time adjusted to the deep gloom of the church. He stood up, seized Veronica's hands and pulled her to her feet. "Come on. We've got to get out of here, and home as quick as we can. And whatever we do we mustn't leave anything behind."

"No, indeed. Someone might guess what we'd been up to, and that would prevent us using it another time, wouldn't it?" Veronica said blithely. "But I'm not moving till I've been thoroughly kissed again."

David was already searching for his clothes, but he complied with her request. In the confined space it was difficult for them both to move, find their garments and dress, especially as they could only use the torch sparingly in case someone passing might see an unusual glow of light in the church. They kept on bumping into each other, and the process was not helped by Veronica's constant giggling, and her refusal to take their situation seriously. Then she couldn't find her bag, and while looking for it David dropped the torch and had difficulty in making it work again. But at last they were ready to go, and began to grope their way down the steep steps from the organ loft.

They smelt smoke as soon as they emerged from the side door of the church. David locked the door and, burdened with pillows and the blanket, they hurried to the car. They had parked on the lane which led to Church Cottage, and here the smell was stronger. It was a cold clear night with a slight breeze that seemed to blow the smoke in their direction. They sniffed anxiously.

"Something's on fire," Veronica said as they bundled their belongings into the Mini. "David, I think it might be Church Cottage."

"So do I." David paused, then "Payne!" he exclaimed.

He started to run, followed by Veronica. As soon as the cottage came in sight, it was obvious that a fierce fire was raging in at least one room. The curtains of the sitting-room had been closed, but one had already caught alight and was burning, making a gap through which they could see flickers of flame.

It was through this gap that, when they reached the cottage, David was able to peer into the room. At first he could see nothing through the thick smoke inside. Then some quirk in the currents of air caused the smoke to clear partially and, by the light of the fire itself, he saw a dark form lying on the floor, beside what seemed to be an overturned wooden chair. The next moment the scene was hidden again, but the glimpse had been sufficient.

"Payne *is* in there. I'm going in. Try to get him out. You get to the Brevints and phone for help."

"David, you can't. You'll be killed." Veronica seized his arm, but he shrugged her off angrily.

"Don't be a fool! I must! Fire brigade. Doctor. Ambulance. Police. Get help! Run, Veronica, damn you! Run!"

Veronica wasn't used to taking orders from David, nor to being sworn at. On most occasions it was she who took the initiative. But now she obeyed without question. She tore down the lane, kicking off her second shoe as soon as she lost her first, and arrived at the old vicarage, heart pounding, chest heaving, catching her breath in great gulps. She didn't think she had ever run so fast in her life. Plenty of exercise this evening, she thought irrelevantly as she put her thumb on the bell-push and kept it there. She could hear the bell ringing but, not satisfied, began to hammer on the door with her fist as well.

David Walden was no fool. He was sensible and level-headed and had no lack of physical courage. He had sized up the situation rapidly, and knew what he had to do if there were to be the faintest hope of saving the parson.

Tearing off his coat as he went, he raced around the side of the cottage to where he remembered there was a rain-water butt. He had been wearing a scarf, and he plunged it into the water before tying it tightly around his mouth and nose. Then he immersed the coat. There was no time to let it soak thoroughly but, thrown round his shoulders, it would afford him some protection.

He ran back to the front of the cottage. He tried the door, but as he had expected, it was locked. There was nothing for it but to break a window—but with what? Conveniently, the border of the small lawn in front of the cottage was edged with granite boulders of a reasonable size, so, thankful that he was wearing gloves, he chose a window furthest from the burning curtain and punched at the glass with all the force he could command.

The window cracked and broke at once, but David found it was not so easy to make a space large enough for him to get through without major injury. But he was conscious of time passing and realized he could delay no longer. He dropped the boulder and climbed into the room. He could see nothing. The heat was intense, and the scarf was drying rapidly and becoming less effective than he had hoped; smoke began to fill his nostrils.

He dropped to the floor where the air was slightly clearer, and crawled towards the door of the sitting-room, near where he had seen Payne lying. To his surprise he became entangled in what seemed to be a chair and a length of rope. Freeing himself, he felt Payne's body to one side of him. There was no possibility of picking him up and carrying him. He must be dragged into the hall and—if the front door opened readily enough—to safety.

David was already having difficulty breathing, but he somehow managed to get his arms under Payne's shoulders and pull him along the carpet. Kneeling, he opened the door of the sitting-room, and immediately there was some relief as the smoke billowed into the hall and thinned slightly.

Then, as David was feeling more hopeful, a stupid but apparently insurmountable problem arose. Payne's body refused to come through the doorway. His head and shoulders were in the hall, but his lower half seemed somehow to be wedged in what should have been a more than adequate space.

David had to climb back over him to find the obstruction,

and it took him several more seconds to free Payne's legs from the rope and the chair with which they seemed to be tangled. But at last David and his burden reached the front door. He got it open more easily than he had expected, felt the wonderful rush of fresh air, gave a final heave to what he was sure must be the parson's lifeless body, and collapsed across it.

And, as he heard steps pounding down the lane and saw lights approaching, he realized he was safe and wasn't going to die. He found himself grinning inanely. He shifted his weight, and a sound—half sigh, half groan—came from beneath him. He rolled off Payne, suddenly aware that the parson, too, was alive.

He put his face close to Payne's. "You're all right," he said. "Help's coming. Don't worry."

David's voice emerged as little more than a croak, and it was clear that if Payne had heard what had been said, the words meant nothing to him. Indeed, David doubted whether he was fully conscious, but nevertheless he was muttering something. David bent closer and said, "Everything's all right, Father Payne. Don't worry."

Payne's lids fluttered and his eyes opened. He sighed and muttered again. To David, what he was saying sounded like "anger" or "angst," and then, "no, no." Finally Payne sighed again.

At that moment Veronica returned, and with her Colonel Brevint, equipped with a fire extinguisher. David staggered to his feet, to be almost knocked down again as Veronica threw herself at him and embraced him.

"Thank God!" she said breathlessly. "Oh, thank God!"

The Colonel was on his knees beside Payne. "He's still alive, just, I think," he said. "Help me to move him away from the house if you can, Walden. Can't manage it on my own. Dorothy's phoning all the right bods. They'll be here soon."

The next few minutes were confused. Dorothy Brevint drove up in their station wagon with another fire extinguisher and some blankets. She had phoned the fire brigade and Dr. Band, but inevitably they would take some time to arrive. She had also roused Tom Cresford, the verger, as well as a neighbour, who had in turn roused others, so that there were many willing hands to lift Father Payne into the back of the station wagon and take him and David to the old vicarage. Meanwhile, some of the men were doing their best with extinguishers and buckets of water. In addition, Dorothy Brevint had called Sir William and Lady Gerart, to tell them what had happened, but that their daughter was safe. They were on their way.

Once at the vicarage, David Walden tried to avoid thinking of his efforts to save Father Payne. He was thankful to be alive, and for the moment that was sufficient. The Brevints couldn't have been kinder. When David maintained that what he wanted was to get out of his horrible smelly clothes, have a shower, wash his hair and rid himself of the stench of smoke, Colonel Brevint insisted on standing by to help him. The result was that he was soon huddled in an armchair in front of a big electric fire in the Brevints' sitting-room, wrapped in a blanket and wearing a pair of pyjamas much too small for him. He still felt shocked and exhausted, and he shivered occasionally and hawked into tissues the Brevints had provided, while Veronica brought him cups of hot, sweet tea. She insisted that tea was better than whisky for shock, and refused to answer any questions about the progress of the fire.

Eventually, however, his mind began to clear. He remembered the rope entangled around the parson's legs and around the chair. It had been a wooden chair, a kitchen chair, he recalled. What was it doing in Payne's sitting-room? And what was Payne doing there that he had allowed himself to be overcome by smoke before he could escape from the house? Had he been asleep? There had been no lights on. And how had the fire started?

He was interrupted by Dorothy Brevint, who brought in Dr. Band. "Here he is, Doctor," she said. "The hero of the occasion. He really was extraordinarily brave."

"So I gather." Band grinned at David Walden, who flushed as he realized that Mrs. Brevint was talking about him. "And how is the hero?" the doctor went on. "Let's have a look at you, Mr. Walden. The ambulance has just arrived, so if necessary we can whisk you off to hospital."

"No, I'm fine. I swallowed a little smoke, that's all," David protested. "I certainly don't need to go to hospital. Anyway, what about Father Payne? You've seen him? Shouldn't he be on his way?"

Dr. Band glanced at Dorothy Brevint and Veronica as he rummaged in his little black bag. He seemed to take an inordinate amount of time to find his stethoscope, and even longer to answer Walden's question. At last he said, "Yes, I've seen Payne. I told them not to tell you immediately, and I'm sorry to add another shock, but all your good work was in vain. Mr. Payne is dead. He was dead when I arrived."

"Dead? Oh no! I'm so sorry," David said.

Mrs. Brevint was tactfully urging Veronica out of the room so that the doctor could examine David. As she went, she said, "Poor Father Payne! We're all so sorry. And of course there's the feast tomorrow—today now. We must discuss the arrangements as soon as your parents arrive, Veronica . . ."

Her voice was cut off as the door was shut behind them, leaving Dr. Band and David Walden alone. The doctor began his examination. It didn't take long.

"You're fine," he said. "A healthy young man—and sensible. If you'd not taken the precautions I've been told about you might not have got off so lightly."

"But it took time. Perhaps if I'd been quicker—"

"No! I very much doubt if a couple of minutes would have made any difference, Mr. Walden—to Payne, that is. All that might have happened is that we'd probably have had two bodies on our hands instead of one. Incidentally," Dr. Band continued smoothly, "you'll be glad to know that the fire is under control, though the brigade will stay around damping it down. There's been a lot of damage, of course, from smoke and water, but it's mainly confined to the sitting-room. The whole place might have been gutted if you and Miss Gerart hadn't happened to be passing."

"I—I wasn't exactly passing—" David Walden began, and stopped.

Here was a complication that hadn't occurred to him before. How was he to explain that he and Veronica had "happened" to be passing near Church Cottage at that time of night? They had gone to the church ostensibly to find Veronica's bracelet, but they couldn't pretend to have spent hours looking for it. And the Gerarts' interrogation could not be long delayed. David closed his eyes and, opening them again, found the doctor frowning at him.

"You're not feeling so good? Perhaps you'd better go and have some oxygen."

"No, I'm OK, really, Doctor. I'm just a bit tired," David said, and thought he had better keep his mouth shut until he had had a chance to compare notes with Veronica.

"Very well. But I'd advise you to get to your own bed as soon as possible and have a good sleep," said Band. "Would you like a sedative?"

"No, thank you, Doctor."

Dr. Band nodded. "Fine. Then I'll send off the ambulance, and see if anyone else needs my ministrations. Good night."

"Good night, Doctor, and thank you."

For a few blissful minutes David Walden was alone. He found his strength returning, and his mind becoming normally active as he tried to piece together the events at the cottage. Then suddenly the room seemed to be full of people— Veronica, the Brevints and, unexpectedly, John Courtney, proudly waving a bandaged hand to show that he had done his bit by helping to put the fire out. Sir William and Lady Gerart had arrived at the old vicarage a little earlier, and were just being ushered into the room. Walden made an effort to stand up, but was hampered by the blanket.

"Sit down, my dear fellow. Sit down," Sir William commanded.

"David, how are you? Veronica's been telling me how very brave you were to try to save poor Father Payne," said Lady Gerart.

"Damn brave!" the Colonel echoed emphatically. "I wouldn't have liked to go into that burning room to rescue anyone, not even my nearest and dearest."

"I quite agree," said Sir William. "You did well, David. Incidentally," he went on, "we guessed the state you must be in, and Lady Gerart packed a few of your own clothes for you. I'm sure Dorothy will let you go and change whenever you like. Then you can get home to bed."

"Thanks a lot for thinking of that, Sir William. But I really am all right. Just a bit tired, as I told the doctor. It was the smoke that—that made things difficult." David was embarrassed by the sudden attention. Nevertheless, his new-found reputation for courage seemed to have distracted the Gerarts' attention from inquiries about their daughter's presence with him at the scene. Or had Veronica already . . . "I'm only sorry that Father Payne hasn't survived," he added.

Lady Gerart had begun to talk earnestly with the Brevints about what was to happen to St. Blaise's Feast now they had no priest. Behind them Veronica gave David a broad wink. Sir William was frowning.

"What I don't understand," he said, "is why Payne, who was a perfectly able-bodied young man, didn't dash out of the cottage. Even if he'd tried to put out the fire he wouldn't have been overcome by smoke so quickly as to prevent him escaping. After all, David wasn't." Sir William shook his head. "I suppose he could have fallen asleep in an armchair. But he was on the ground floor and in a familiar place. He knew where the door was and everything else."

"It's a mystery," said John Courtney with some relish, "but doubtless one the police and the fire people will solve when they start asking their questions."

"There's another aspect to it, too," said David quietly. "I wouldn't swear that Father Payne had been tied to a chair, but in retrospect I rather think he was."

The others stared at him as he continued. "Certainly there was a chair, a wooden one, the kind you have in a kitchen, not a sitting-room. I caught a glimpse of it, overturned beside him, before I climbed into the room. And when I was trying to pull him through the door, I was hampered by the chair, which was entangled with his legs and a rope."

"The mystery deepens," said John Courtney.

He seemed to be the only one who was getting any pleasure from David's disclosures. The others were either puzzled, disbelieving or merely amazed. Walden had the impression that they were looking at him as if he were somehow responsible.

"Why should anyone tie Father Payne to a chair and then leave him to die a horrible death?" Lady Gerart voiced what they were all thinking.

"I haven't the faintest idea," David Walden said desperately. "And I told you I couldn't swear to it. It may not have been like that at all. I was blinded with the smoke. I could hardly see. Breathing was getting difficult. I could have got the picture all wrong. But somehow I don't think so."

"It would explain why Payne couldn't escape," Sir William said.

"True," said Colonel Brevint. Then, "I suppose it could have been would-be thieves, or more likely vandals. There wasn't much to steal at Church Cottage."

"Perhaps they were after St. Blaise's silver," Courtney suggested mildly. "Those candlesticks alone would be worth a few pounds if you knew where to sell them."

There was a horrified silence. Then everyone spoke at once. Sir William quelled the din by insisting that there was only one thing to do—check if the silver was still in the church. But this proved to be less simple than it sounded.

When the Church of St. Blaise was locked up, the big main doors were bolted from the inside. Entrance and exit were then by the side door, the door that Veronica and David had used earlier that night, or by a door into the vestry. Only Payne and Cresford, the verger, had keys to the vestry. The side door had three keys. Again the parson and the verger had one each, while the third was kept at the Manor.

"You've got our key, Veronica," said Lady Gerart.

"No. David has it," Veronica replied. "He locked the door when we came out."

"It's in my coat pocket," Walden said.

Mrs. Brevint went off to the kitchen where David's dirty wet clothes had been taken. She returned, shaking her head. The key wasn't there. It must have fallen out of David's pocket in the confusion, which meant it might be anywhere, in the water-butt, in the front garden of the cottage, inside the burnt-out sitting-room.

"We'll have to get Tom Cresford's key," Sir William said. "Come on, Jack. We'll take my car. It'll be quicker. We'll be back as soon as we can—with good news, we hope. David, you're beginning to look as if you could do with a good sleep. I suggest that Veronica take you back to the Manor. You wait here, Constance, if Dorothy doesn't mind."

Cresford lived at the further end of Fairfield. He had just got home from the scene of the fire and was making himself a cup of tea when Sir William and the Colonel arrived, but when they said they needed to check on the church silver, he insisted on accompanying them.

"You mean you think the fire might not have been an accident, Sir William?" he said as they drove through the village, where more lights were showing than was usual at that time of the morning. "But that's dreadful. Poor Father Payne. Who'd do such a wicked thing?"

"We don't know, Cresford. We're guessing. There may be nothing to it," said Sir William. "If the silver's safe . . ."

He drew up beside the church. John Courtney, apparently determined not to be left out, was waiting for them at the side door. But it was Cresford who produced the key and took charge. He opened the door and, turning on the lights as he went, led the way to the Lady Chapel. Everything seemed to be in order; there was no sign of any disturbance.

Cresford bent and pushed the stone that opened the wall section. Behind him there was an audible sigh of relief as the two bags were revealed.

"Thank God for that," said Sir William. "At least it's one mercy."

"Hadn't you better look inside?" Courtney remarked. "You might have been left bags of stones."

Sir William glared at him, but nevertheless with Cresford's help he pulled out the bags and opened them. Together they checked on the contents. As far as they could tell, the silver was intact.

"Well done, Father Payne!" said Colonel Brevint suddenly. "He never told them where the silver was. The man was a hero—a martyr, in fact, like his namesake."

Sir William, Courtney and Cresford stared at the Colonel in surprise.

"Well, isn't it obvious?" Brevint said. "The would-be thieves must have tried to force Father Payne to tell them where the silver was—"

Sir William intervened. "That's just a guess, Jack. Cresford, you're not to mention this idea, not to anyone, at least for the moment, there's a good chap. Doubtless the police will be able to tell us what happened."

"Yes, Sir William," said Cresford, wondering what his wife would have to say about this interesting news. Then, without asking for permission, he heaved the bags back into the hidey-hole and closed the door.

CHAPTER 13

Normally a fire in a Cotswold village, even one resulting in a death, would have failed to cause more than the gentlest of ripples at the Kidlington headquarters of the Thames Valley Police. Of course, there would have to be an investigation, in conjunction with the fire service, just as there would have to be an inquest. But from the point of view of the police, the matter would probably have been handled by a detective-sergeant if not a uniformed officer, and would certainly have been unlikely to come to the attention of the Serious Crime Squad.

But this fire and this death were different. It was Dr. Band who was the first to sound an official alarm. He had been alerted by a pair of astute ambulance men, who had inadvertently uncovered the body's feet while arranging it in the ambulance, and had seen that they were bare. This had surprised them, as otherwise the corpse was fully clothed. Then they had noticed the strange marks on the soles of the feet, and had drawn Dr. Band's attention to them.

"Funny, those, aren't they, Doctor?" one of them had commented uneasily. "They look like little burns made by a cigarette, but how the devil—"

Band, who completely agreed with this immediate diagnosis and was kicking himself for not having noticed the marks when he was making sure that life was extinct, interrupted the ambulance man. "We'd better wait to hear what the pathologist has to report," he said firmly, squashing further surmise. But when he got home he spent a little time considering the situation before telephoning the police headquarters at Kidlington and leaving a message with the duty officer for Detective Chief Inspector Tansey to call him back as soon as possible.

As a result, by 8:00 A.M. that Sunday morning the chief inspector and Sergeant Greenway were on their way to Fairfield. They went first to Church Cottage. Here they found a police constable doing his best to keep control of a collection of curious villagers—mainly small boys—while there remained at the scene two firemen with a salvage appliance. A reporter from the *Oxford Mail* had arrived, and his photographer was already at work.

Tansey introduced himself and his sergeant, though it was unnecessary. The reporter had recognized him at once, and demanded a statement. Why should a senior officer be interested in a village fire? There had been a death, but was there any suspicion of foul play? A rumour was going around that thieves had been after the church silver. Was there any truth in it? Was there any connection with the body found in Copley Wood a few weeks ago?

Tansey listened to this string of questions, and answered them quite simply and cheerfully. "I've no idea," he said. "Indeed you seem to know more about the matter than I do. So, if you'll let us get on with our job—"

With a dismissive wave of his hand, Tansey strode up to the cottage with the senior fireman and peered through the broken window into the sitting-room. "Not too good, is it, sir?" said the man. "We did our best to keep down the damage, but by the time we got here—well, you can see. Our chief officer from Colombury's on his way here to meet you, according to our last radio message. He wants to start the investigation today."

The sitting-room was indeed a sorry spectacle. The room was black and filthy, smoke-grimed and sodden with water. An occasional table had been knocked over, and the flowers which had presumably stood on it were scattered on the carpet. Near the door was what appeared to be a broken chair. The smell, a mixture of damp and smoke, was enough to make both the chief inspector and his sergeant wrinkle their noses.

"How much have you had to disturb in here?" he asked the fireman quickly.

"Very little in this room, beyond making sure it was safe," replied the man. "By the time we got here the room was burnt out, almost as you see it. We concentrated on preventing the fire spreading to the rest of the place."

"Good," said Tansey. "We'll go in, if that's all right."

"Oh yes, sir. The structure's perfectly sound."

The front door was open and, accompanied by both the firemen, they stepped through it. The fire had hardly affected the hall, though some smoke and water damage was evident. But the stench was strong. Tansey produced a handkerchief to hold over his nose, and motioned to Greenway to do the same as they went into the sitting-room.

Inadvertently Tansey kicked the broken chair, and bent down to examine it. The rope that had been attached to it was largely charred, and disintegrated when he touched it with a finger, though there was absolutely no doubt what it was. Tansey was not surprised. Dr. Band had said that the only explanation he could imagine for the state of the Reverend Blaise Payne's feet was that they had been deliberately burnt by a lighted cigarette, and the parson would hardly have let that happen unless he had been restrained in some way.

"There are no obvious signs of a struggle," remarked Tansey, "though it's damned difficult to tell in this setting. As far as one can guess, Payne either knew his attacker, or was overpowered very quickly. But we're going to need a lot more detail before we can be sure."

"Such as why anyone should want to tie Father Payne up, and torture him," said Greenway.

"Yes, if that's really what happened." Tansey was studying the room. "OK. We'd better go into action. It looks as if Band was right. Treat it as a case of murder. Get down to the car and tell HQ to warn the pathologist and get a scene of crime team out here immediately. Then we'll go off to the Manor and talk to David Walden, who tried to rescue Payne."

He turned to the senior fireman. "In the meantime, until we can get more men here, I'd be glad if you'd both help the constable keep everyone away—and don't touch anything else yourselves unless you have to. And don't mention the possibility of murder to anyone, either—especially not that reporter."

"Very good, sir," said the fireman. "We understand."

"And when your chief officer arrives he can liaise with the scene of crime inspector, who should be along within the hour. I'll see them both later in the day."

"Yes, sir," said the fireman.

"What is it, Constable?" The officer who had been on duty outside had come into the room. The chief inspector repeated the instructions he had given to the firemen. "The important thing is to keep everyone away. We'll send you reinforcements to cordon off the whole area very soon."

"It's all right, sir. Those people are only locals, so far. They'll do as they're told. But you're wanted on your car phone, sir."

"Coming." Greenway ran.

When Tansey joined her, she said, "The call's from Kidlington, sir. Sir William Gerart's phoned them direct. He'd like to see a senior police officer as soon as possible, about Father Payne and the fire—and the church silver."

"The church silver?" Tansey shrugged. "All right, Sergeant, thanks." He took the instrument from her. "Tansey here." He paused and listened. Then he said, "There's no doubt, I'm afraid. I'm on my way to Sir William Gerart—and the chap who discovered the fire. Now—" He gave his orders.

In spite of the fact that they had had very little sleep the previous night, the inhabitants of the Manor had all assembled in the dining-room for breakfast by about 8:45 A.M. on St. Blaise's Feast Day. Even David Walden had made the effort, in spite of protestations that he should rest a little longer in bed before he had to play the organ at the service.

In fact, Sir William and Lady Gerart had been in action for some time before that. Constance was not one to let grass grow under her feet, and in any case there was a great deal to be done. They couldn't afford to waste time, however tempting that idea might be.

The early communion service had inevitably been cancelled, and matins postponed for half an hour. Sir William had affixed a large notice to this effect on the church door before leaving the previous night to snatch what sleep he could. And Colonel Brevint had volunteered to be on guard at the church to offer an explanation to those who knew nothing of the events of the night, or of Father Payne's death.

The members of the Parochial Church Council had already been peremptorily woken from their sleep by Lady Gerart, and told the news. Cutting short their expressions of horror, she had obtained general agreement with the plan that matins —or at least a service of some kind—should be held at eleven-thirty. The lunch would follow, as arranged. It was, everyone agreed, what poor Father Payne would have wished. On receiving Lady Gerart's call Miss Mabson had immediately driven over to the Manor to breakfast with the Gerarts, and discuss the form of the service she would have to take.

"We should have a minute of silent prayer in memory of Father Payne," she suggested. Then she added, "I'm terribly sorry for him, of course—and *de mortuis* and all that—but I must admit I shouldn't have expected him to make such a great effort to defend our church silver. Clearly I misjudged the man."

"We don't actually know that's what happened," said Constance Gerart. "It's only surmise. David could have been mistaken about the chair and the rope. Anyway, William has already been on to the police, and we should wait for them. Best not to mention any suspicions publicly."

"Of course not," Jane Mabson agreed.

"William should, I think, make a short innocuous announcement before the service begins," said Lady Gerart.

"That would be best," said Miss Mabson. "Then the silent prayer, followed by a service that shouldn't be too mournful. We've much to be thankful for—"

David Walden, who had been called from the room a few moments before, returned looking exasperated. "That was a reporter," he said, "wanting to know my feelings as I was rescuing Father Payne."

"Why not?" said Veronica. "You're a hero, David."

"Nonsense! I told him anyone would have done the same, and then I realized what an awful cliché that was. But what on earth does one say?"

"You'd better think of something," said Sir William. "There may be quite a lot of publicity if Payne was—was murdered. It won't be altogether pleasant, either, for any of us. The village will be filled with police and photographers and all the trappings."

There was a silence while they contemplated the future. Then Sir William finished his coffee, wiped his mouth on his table napkin and stood up. "And now, if you'll excuse me," he said, "I'll make yet another effort to get hold of Theo Payne's secretary up in the North, and incidentally tell Church House at North Hinksey. I'd like them all to be warned before the police arrive on the doorstep or they hear it on the radio. David, if you feel up to it, you'd better come and help."

"Oh dear!" Lady Gerart sighed. "This was going to be such a happy day—and now—"

"Yes, well—about the service," said Miss Mabson, determined to be practical.

But again she was interrupted, this time by Sir William, who returned to the dining-room. "At last I got hold of Bishop Payne's secretary," he said. "He was dreadfully shocked, naturally. As we guessed, Theo is already on his way to Africa on some kind of pastoral visit, but the secretary will try to get hold of him. In the meantime, the poor devil had to break the news to Theo's wife, Mary."

"At least that'll be better than hearing about it from a stranger," said Lady Gerart. "What exactly did you tell him, William?"

"What we agreed," he said. "There's been a fire at Church Cottage. As yet, we have no idea how it started. Father Payne had been saved from the place by the bravery of David Walden, my secretary, but had died subsequently. I didn't mention the silver, or anything else, and I said we'd keep in close touch. That's all we can do for the moment."

"But if they get hold of the bishop he's sure to phone us, even from Africa," said Lady Gerart. "What do we say then? And what about that sister? Surely she should be told."

"I suspect Theo will phone. But we must stick to the same story." Her husband was definite. "It's no use speculating till we have some facts. In any case it's a job for the police and the fire people—not for us. As for the sister, we've no means of tracing her whereabouts. That'll be up to the authorities, too, if Mary Payne doesn't know where she is; Father Payne said she'd gone to London, but . . ."

CHAPTER 14

"What we need are some facts, and we wouldn't mind hearing a little gossip," said Chief Inspector Tansey. "It doesn't matter how trivial something may seem. At this point in an inquiry anything could turn out to be useful."

He looked hopefully from Sir William Gerart to David Walden; his primary interest at present was in Walden, but Sir William had insisted on being present during the interview. They were in the Gerarts' small sitting-room, and the atmosphere was informal. But Walden seemed a little tense. He had glanced several times at Sergeant Greenway, who was sitting unobtrusively at one side of the room, her notebook open on her lap.

"Perhaps, Mr. Walden, you'd first tell me in your own words what you know of the events of last night, and exactly what part you played in them," Tansey said. "Then I expect I shall have some questions for you."

"Yes," said Walden. He had managed a few words alone with Veronica, and they had agreed on how to account for the missing hours, when in fact they had been making love or asleep afterwards on the floor of the organ loft. But he knew their story—the best they could devise at short notice—was pretty implausible, and felt it might ring less false if Sir William were not present to judge it.

"Well," he started again. "It was like this. I'd never have been anywhere near Church Cottage if Miss Gerart hadn't lost a gold bracelet of which she was particularly fond. She was sure she'd dropped it in the church during the day, and thought she knew exactly where. She wasn't very keen on going over there by herself in the dark, and asked me—"

Tansey listened attentively, occasionally nodding encouragement when Walden hesitated. He noted the discrepancy in the timings, the unbelievably long period spent searching for the bracelet and chatting in the Mini after they had found it, but made no comment. For the moment, he was more interested in the actual fire and the events that had taken place at the cottage.

"What was your first impression when you looked through that sitting-room window, Mr. Walden?" he asked.

"I couldn't see much. There was a lot of smoke and, in spite of the flames, it was pretty dark."

"The curtains were drawn, you said—except for the gap the fire had burnt in them. Were the lights on or off?"

"Off. But for a moment or so the smoke seemed to clear and I saw Father Payne lying on the floor, not too far from the door to the hall, as if he'd collapsed before he'd got there." Walden was becoming more confident now, Tansey noted. "Payne seemed to be tangled up in something like a chair. It wasn't till I was actually inside and had difficulty pulling him through the door that I realized it was indeed a chair, a wooden kitchen chair, and there was a bit of rope tangled round both him and the chair. On reflection, I'm pretty sure he'd been tied up."

"Did you notice his feet?"

"Feet?" The question surprised Walden, who frowned. "His feet? You mean what sort of shoes he was wearing? No, Chief Inspector, I paid no attention to his feet. Should I have done?"

Tansey didn't answer. And Sir William, who had scarcely spoken until now, intervened to mention the church silver, and outline the theory that Father Payne had refused, even under threats of violence—or perhaps actual violence—to reveal its hiding-place.

"At least if he were tied up, it would explain why he

couldn't simply run out of the cottage," he said. "Though why the would-be thieves should set fire to the place and leave him to die I can't imagine."

"Presumably he'd have recognized them again," Walden said.

"Yes, but what of it? They probably threatened him, possibly used violence," said Sir William, "but as crimes go these days that sort of thing's not all that serious. Now, without getting what they'd hoped for, they've committed arson and murder. It was a mad way to act. I don't understand it."

Nor did Tansey, who had been listening to this exchange of views in silence. The question had already occurred to him, and so far he had reached no plausible answer. Professionals didn't usually commit unnecessary crimes, and amateurs hardly went around planting lighted cigarettes on people's bare feet. He was assuming that Dr. Band was right, of course . . .

"Would you know if Mr. Payne had any enemies?" he asked.

Both Sir William and Walden shook their heads, and Sir William said, "I suppose we could be quite wrong about the silver, but there's nothing worth stealing at Church Cottage. There are lots of houses, even in the village, where they'd have done better. And, as for enemies, it seems absurd. He'd only been here a few weeks. Unless, of course, they were villains he'd crossed in his last parish, in the East End of London. There was something an acquaintance of mine said at a dinner party here last Saturday—" Sir William hesitated.

"Yes?" prompted the chief inspector.

"Well, it's really hearsay—at two removes," said Sir William. "You should ask Simon Ashe himself about it. But apparently he met a barrister friend of his in London who had once prosecuted a known prostitute for theft. Father Payne gave evidence for the defence—evidence which got her off. Ashe said his friend told him the girl was guilty as hell, and wondered if Payne had given false evidence to save her. But, as I say, you must get the details from Ashe."

"Indeed I will," said Tansey.

There was a long pause, each of the three men busy with his own thoughts. The silence was broken by Walden, who suddenly asked, "Has anyone thought of vandals—burning the cottage, I mean?"

"Surely not," Sir William objected. "Apples get stolen and there's an occasional stone through a window, but this is a surprisingly peaceful community. And if you're thinking of that motorcycle gang that terrorized us last midsummer's night, David, they've never been back, and anyway you and Veronica would have heard them, wouldn't you?"

Tansey coughed behind his hand to hide his smile as Walden flushed at this seemingly innocent question. Sir William, he thought, might not have made a great impression in the House of Commons, but he wasn't a fool. He clearly didn't believe that his daughter and David Walden had spent quite so much time just sitting in the Mini, talking to each other.

The chief inspector thought it best to change the subject. "I appreciate that you didn't know Mr. Payne very well, but you must have formed some opinion of his character. Would you have said he was a courageous man, brave enough to allow himself to be knocked about a little rather than disclose where the silver was hidden?"

"But was he? Knocked about?" Sir William asked.

"Not that I saw," Walden said.

"Please. You've not answered my question," said Tansey.

"Sorry, Chief Inspector, but you must know it's not easy to make a guess at how men will react under stress." Sir William hesitated; he didn't like passing judgement on a dead man, but he had to answer the question. "On the whole, he struck me as being pretty strong-minded, though he didn't always give that impression. But whether he'd have thought the silver worth suffering for, I rather doubt, and you can't blame him. What do you think, David?"

"I agree, Sir William."

"Another point then, Mr. Walden, and please consider your answer carefully," said Tansey. "The rope that was attached to the chair is very charred by now. When you were trying to free Mr. Payne this wouldn't have been the case. So, did you have much difficulty freeing him?"

David Walden screwed up his eyes in thought, reliving the long minute he had struggled in that hot, smoke-filled room before he managed to release Payne. "It wasn't easy, certainly," he said slowly. "The rope was all tangled up with the chair and Father Payne, as I said, and of course I couldn't see what I was doing. But it wasn't tied tightly. There were no knots to undo, or I couldn't have managed it. I think that perhaps if he'd had more time before he was overcome he might have freed himself."

Tansey was saved from comment by a tap at the door and the entry of Veronica. The men looked at her inquiringly.

"Sorry to interrupt," she said, "but Bishop Payne's on the phone from Africa, Dad, wanting to speak to you."

Sir William leapt to his feet. "Oh God!" he said, grimacing. "That was quick of them. Excuse me, Chief Inspector. This is difficult. You've been told our Father Payne is Bishop Payne's nephew?"

"Of course, sir." Tansey also stood up and, as Sir William left the room, gestured to Veronica to remain. "Miss Gerart, if you wouldn't mind."

Veronica glanced at David and smiled at Tansey. "Questions?" she said. "I doubt if I can tell you more than David has. He was the brave one, dashing into that burning building. I merely ran down the lane to the Brevints and got them to phone for help."

"Miss Gerart, will you please tell me what time you first smelt smoke, and realized that Church Cottage was on fire?"

"It must have been about eleven-thirty."

"We have a record of when Mrs. Brevint called the fire brigade and the doctor. It was after midnight." Both Veronica and David were silent, and Tansey continued. "Surely you understand that the point is important. We need to know all the relevant timings, so that the fire officers and I can try to gauge when the fire was started. It had got a good hold by the time you reached it, Mr. Walden, but if you'd been sitting in the car as you said, wouldn't you have smelt the smoke before?"

Walden nodded miserably. "All right, Chief Inspector. I suspect you've guessed. We were in the church, not in the car. We were up in the organ loft for quite a time. We came out of the side door at about twelve, I think, and smelt the smoke immediately. It was quite strong."

"Thank you. Then am I right to assume you wouldn't have heard a car passing in the lane?"

Veronica looked at David. "Yes, you are," she said, grinning cheerfully. "We were otherwise engaged. And, even when we got outside the church we didn't hear either a car or anyone until—until people arrived to help."

Tansey nodded. Then he said suddenly, "What was your opinion of Mr. Payne, Miss Gerart?"

"I couldn't make up my mind," she replied frankly. "He wasn't unattractive, but there was something off-putting about him. I couldn't really place him as a simple country parson, and of course it's true that he'd only served in the East End of London—that is, until he took those months off to look after his sister, Kay."

"Ah yes," said Tansey, "we've heard of his sister. Tell me about her."

"Well," said Veronica, "she was a super-glamorous character. Some people—Miss Mabson, for instance—took an instant dislike to her. Personally, I found her—intriguing. She wasn't what you'd expect, but then we gather she'd had a kind of breakdown and was recuperating."

"Where was she during the fire? Where is she now?" asked Tansey.

"We've no idea. She suddenly decided on Saturday to go to London, I gather. Father Payne had to drive her into Oxford, and that made him late for a dinner party here. We were just saying that it would be a matter for the police to find her and tell her the news about her brother—Billy, as she called him—if Mrs. Payne, her aunt, doesn't know where she is."

"I see," said Tansey slowly. He had listened with interest to what Veronica had said about Payne, and his background, and his sister.

Veronica added, "But, whatever one thought of Billy, you can't get away from the fact that he was pretty brave if he was trying to save that silver. It's more than I'd have done in his place. To be honest, I don't understand it, unless he didn't believe they were going to set fire to the cottage—or he was sure he could escape before there was any real danger."

"If only we'd gone there a bit earlier—" Walden said.

"Perhaps it was fortunate for you that you didn't," said Tansey. "You might have run into whoever was—was attacking Mr. Payne."

Veronica shivered. "Heaven forbid! Incidentally, Chief Inspector, you should ask my mother—and Jane Mabson—what they thought of Father Payne. They knew him better than anyone else, though that's not saying much—I mean, I guess he wasn't an easy man to know. Or am I being stupid?"

"You've been a great help, Miss Gerart," Tansey said. "And I'm certainly going to speak to your mother. Would you ask her if she could spare me a few minutes?"

"Of course," said Veronica, and as she and Walden reached the door, she turned and beamed at Tansey before adding, "We hope you won't find it necessary to mention the—the organ loft, Chief Inspector. I'm sure you understand."

"I doubt if I will, Miss Gerart," said Tansey as he returned her smile.

Lady Gerart arrived so promptly that the two detectives had no time to discuss the interviews. She sat down and, having expressed conventional but apparently genuine regret at the death of Father Payne, immediately looked at the clock on the mantel.

"I have to get along to the church as soon as possible," she said. "The early communion was cancelled, of course, but we're having a service and a parish luncheon afterwards. Obviously some reorganization is necessary as we no longer have a priest."

"I'll be as quick as I can, Lady Gerart," said Tansey. "We hope you'll be able to tell us something about Mr. Payne—what sort of man he was, for instance."

"I don't understand—" she began. But Constance Gerart was far from stupid, and after a few moments' consideration while Tansey remained silent she went on, "Ah, now I see your point. Would I be right in thinking you don't necessarily believe he was trying to save—or indeed succeeded in saving—the church silver? You're suggesting that what happened was connected in some way with—with something he was doing before he came to Fairfield, when he was in the East End, perhaps . . ."

"What do you think yourself, Lady Gerart?"

"The silver was on our minds at once, of course," she answered thoughtfully, "and that's the story that's got around the village. It seems somehow a fitting tale to go with the poor man's death. Personally . . ." she paused.

"You're afraid the truth may not be so palatable, Lady Gerart?"

Lady Gerart made an impatient gesture. "I really don't know. He was Bishop Payne's nephew—Theo Payne is an old friend of my husband—and to some extent we took Blaise Payne on trust. Our church was desperate for a priest and, though he knew little or nothing about work in a country parish, we were glad to have him." She paused again, and sighed. "It seems dreadful to suggest it when he's just died, but as the circumstances are so strange—"

"Yes?" prompted Tansey gently.

"Well, Chief Inspector, my husband and I felt we should think twice, as it were, before suggesting that he become our permanent vicar. I can't put my finger on any genuine reason, except that he was a tense, nervous man, but my husband intended to make some inquiries. He was persuaded to do so mainly because of some remarks that Mr. Ashe made after a dinner party here last Saturday."

"I've heard about the incident," said Tansey.

"I see. Well, I managed to prevent my husband taking any steps till after St. Blaise's Feast Day. Now I suppose it will be up to you."

Seeing her obvious distress, Tansey said, "Lady Gerart, as far as we can tell, it's not impossible that individuals from a previous period of Mr. Payne's life were responsible for his death, but it's much too early to make such an assumption." He paused, and then some quirk made him ask, "Can you really not put your finger on any specific oddity about him?"

It was a moment before Constance Gerart spoke, obviously with some reluctance. "Nothing that would be of any value as —as evidence, but there was an incident when we were all in the church preparing for the feast. We don't get many visitors at this time of year, but two strangers—young people, a man and a girl—came in, in spite of a notice on the door saying the place was closed, and started to walk up the aisle towards Father Payne and Miss Mabson and myself. Miss Mabson went forward to meet them, but for a moment I thought Father Payne recognized them. He looked as if he were badly shaken, almost as if he were going to pass out. He said it was just a chest pain, that he got them sometimes. I tried to make him go and rest, but he refused."

With sudden determination she looked at the time again and stood up. "I'm sorry, but that's all I can tell you, and I must go. I'll send you in some coffee, and if you'd care to come to the service at St. Blaise and the luncheon afterwards you'd be most welcome." She scarcely waited for their thanks before she was gone.

"What a nice woman," Sergeant Greenway said. "But Payne seems to have been an odd character—and his sister, if what we hear of her is to be believed."

"True. I don't know about you, but I find it difficult to take this church silver theory seriously. Personally, I agree with the Gerarts—I'd tell about some silver to avoid being left to burn. He was obviously resisting, but for some completely different reason. If only we knew what . . ."

For a minute Tansey was lost in thought. Then he said, "We'll have coffee. After that we'll go along to Church Cottage and talk to the inspector and the fire officer. Depending on what they can tell us, we might go on to St. Blaise for the service and the lunch. Everyone will be talking about the fire and Father Payne, and we could easily pick up some worthwhile information."

CHAPTER 15

Since the arrival of the chief inspector and Sergeant Greenway in Fairfield, the temperature had suddenly dropped five degrees, the sky had grown darker and fat white flakes of snow were beginning to fall. Greenway shivered as she got into the car beside Tansey. She started the engine at once, but the heater was unable to produce hot air during the short drive back to Church Cottage.

When they got there they found the scene of crime team hard at work. The cottage and the lane and the area immediately surrounding it had been cordoned off, prohibiting access to the side entrance of the church—this morning's congregation would have to use the main door of the church—but the snow was beginning to fall more thickly, and the police officers would soon have to abandon their outdoor search. A constable saluted and lifted the cordon as they turned into the lane, passing a small group of media men standing nearby. The reporters and photographers were so cold and morose that they failed to intercept Tansey and Greenway.

"Tell me," said Tansey, who had been silent since they left the Manor. "Have you been struck by any omission in what people have had to say this morning?"

"Omission?" Greenway took a few moments to park neatly in front of the cottage behind the police mobile incident van; she needed a moment to think. "Are you thinking about the parson's membership of the so-called Nectar and Ambrosia Club, sir?"

"Indirectly, yes," said Tansey. "But what I really had in mind was that no one has suggested that the villain or villains who caused Payne's death might also be responsible for the body in Copley Wood. No one's mentioned Copley Wood, in fact. Sir William made the point that this is a pretty peaceful part of the country, yet he knows perfectly well that it's seen two violent deaths within weeks of each other."

"Copley Wood's not all that close to Fairfield, sir," said Greenway. "It's not part of the village or its immediate neighbourhood. And an impersonal killing of an unidentified man like that is rather different from this dreadful attack on the parson of the local church, even if he's not been here long. I can understand them not linking the events. Why should they?"

"Because there's an obvious connection, Sergeant—and everyone we've talked to knows of it—that silver button found in the wood near the unidentified body. It's surely a considerable coincidence that there should be two completely independent violent deaths, so close in time and place, yet each apparently related to this N & A Club."

Greenway had no time to answer. The scene of crime inspector and the chief fire officer were at the door of the cottage to greet them, and usher them into the incident caravan. Neither was wearing a coat and neither seemed to notice cold, nor, to judge by the fug in the van, heat either. Maybe their varied duties made them immune to both, reflected Greenway.

"Well, sir," said the inspector. "You'll be glad to know we've learnt a fair amount already."

"Good," said Tansey. "Give me the gist of it."

"First, there was no sign of forcible entry. Either the parson let the villains in or he had left the door unlocked and they walked in on him. The latter would appear unlikely because there was nothing to indicate a struggle. The table that was knocked over and the plant on the floor were due to one of the firemen."

"You said villains in the plural? Any evidence for that—other than the fact that one man couldn't have tied him up without considerable resistance. Payne was a big, strong man. Unless he'd been knocked out first, of course. We shan't know about that till after the PM."

"There is a bit of evidence, sir. One of the villagers, who'd been walking his girl home last night, saw a motorbike with a rider on the pillion going hell for leather through Fairfield. He's not sure of the exact time, but he puts it as shortly after eleven. He says his girl is only a kid—I doubt if he's seventeen himself—and her parents insist she should be home by eleven. It's suggestive, don't you agree, sir?"

"No descriptions, I suppose?" asked Tansey.

"Not of the people on the bike." The inspector shook his head sadly. "Motorcycle gear is an almost perfect disguise, you know. You can't even tell sex. All the boy could say was that he got the impression they were of similar build and that the bike was a heavy, powerful machine. Not a great deal of use, I'm afraid, sir."

Tansey shrugged. "Too much to hope for. Tracks?"

"The lane was examined before we brought any vehicles in, and before it started to snow, sir. Nothing significant. Certainly nothing that we can identify as motorbike tracks."

"Anything else?"

"Yes, Chief Inspector." It was the fire officer who answered Tansey. "Something quite interesting. It looks as if the fire might have been accidental, started by a cigarette end not properly stubbed out and dropped on the floor. We're not certain, but it could have set fire to the bottom of a curtain and the flame could then have spread to the loose-cover of the sofa. Incidentally, there were several cigarette butts in the ashtray, though Mrs. Dolbel, the cleaning woman, says the parson didn't smoke, and his sister, who did smoke and was staying here with him, had already left."

Tansey nodded. He didn't mention to the other officers the

use to which the cigarettes had been put. He was thinking that the picture of some of the previous night's events was becoming clearer, and beginning to make some sense. He was fairly sure he could imagine a reasonably comprehensive scenario.

As he visualized it, two people whom Payne knew, and possibly was expecting, had arrived at Church Cottage. The parson had admitted them. They had—either immediately or later—overpowered him, perhaps threatening him with a weapon, and tied him to a kitchen chair. They had come to get information—the answer to some question or questions, presumably. When Payne refused to give it, they had applied a little torture, enough to persuade him to do what they asked, and had subsequently left him to set himself free. He had almost succeeded in doing so when the accidental fire—not part of the original plan—had overtaken him. His assailants had never intended to kill him.

That much was fairly plain. The rest was guesswork. If murder had never been intended, in spite of the fact that Payne presumably knew the villains, they in their turn must have been perfectly sure that Payne would never report the attack; they had some hold over him which was an adequate guarantee he wouldn't betray them.

And one point was for sure, Tansey thought; the information they had come to seek had nothing whatsoever to do with St. Blaise's church silver. It must have been of a different order of importance and, almost certainly, Payne had provided it.

"We've looked into telling the next of kin, sir," said the inspector. "It seems that the local bishop, who incidentally had never met the dead man, has just come back from a trip abroad. He's volunteered to get in touch with his colleague Bishop Payne, Mr. Payne's uncle."

"Bishop Payne is in Africa, but Sir William Gerart has already been in touch with him by phone and passed on the news," said Tansey. "I hope he decides to come home soon. Identification of his nephew isn't a problem, but I suspect I shall need to have a talk with him."

"There's apparently a sister too, sir. According to Mrs. Dolbel, she's been staying here. But doubtless Bishop Payne will contact her and the rest of the family."

Tansey said, "We heard about the sister, and we're trying to trace her through Bishop Payne's secretary or Mrs. Payne. Now, can we go into the cottage? Everyone's finished there?"

Both officers nodded. The inspector said, "Yes, sir. Everything's been done—the search and photographs—but we've left it all in place for you to see. There are one or two oddities, but I guess you'd rather find them for yourselves. There is another point—"

"Yes?" said Tansey.

"The media are around. You probably saw some at the end of the path. At least a couple of photographers, and a number of reporters—one or two from the nationals—asking questions of anyone they can find. We've kept them outside the cordon, of course, and this snow's put them off a bit. But I was pretty well compelled to say you'd have a word when you'd finished here. And I'm afraid the fact that the victim was tied to a chair has leaked, together with the story about the church silver."

"Not to worry," said Tansey. "The silver's perfectly safe. In fact, I rather doubt if it was ever in danger," he added enigmatically.

He turned to Greenway. "Come along, Sergeant. Let's go and inspect the cottage."

Church Cottage revealed very little about the Reverend Blaise Payne that the two detectives hadn't known before. They found the letter from his uncle, and an obviously unfinished answer, in which Payne apologized for his writing, but explained that he had cut his hand badly and the dressing was inhibiting. There was no other personal correspondence and no photographs, except for a very old sepia print of a nondescript kitten, on the back of which someone had written the name "Blodge."

"Our Payne clearly liked to travel light," commented Tansey. A moment later he uttered a sudden exclamation of interest as he took down a heavy volume of sermons. He laughed. "I've just found a bottle of whisky at the back here," he said. "Perhaps the parson was a secret drinker."

"Poor man," said Greenway. "Maybe he knew those characters would turn up sooner or later, and was scared."

"Or maybe he was careful about the impression he made on the locals," Tansey suggested.

As Tansey and Greenway came out of the front door, they were met by an apologetic inspector, who ushered them to the end of the lane, where a uniformed constable was attempting to shepherd a crowd of reporters and photographers. The representatives of the media had multiplied, and were standing in the slushy snow expecting some reward for the discomfort they were suffering.

The police officers were greeted by a barrage of flash bulbs and questions, but Tansey was not forthcoming and there was a certain amount of grumbling.

"Give us a break, Chief Inspector. Is this connected with that body in Copley Wood?"

"Not as far as I know," said Tansey, speaking the literal truth.

"Any idea why Payne was killed?"

"None."

"Have you contacted Payne's girlfriend yet? The one said to be his sister?"

Tansey made no attempt to answer this last question. Followed by Greenway, he returned to their car and got in. They drove the short distance up the lane to the church.

"Lady Gerart warned us that this place was a breeding-ground for rumours," he said, "and I can guess who started that one about the sister. It was Mr. John Courtney, I'd say. He hinted much the same to me."

"Could there be any truth in it, sir?" Greenway asked.

"Who knows?" said Tansey. "Certainly, bishop's nephew or not, there's no doubt the Reverend Blaise Payne was no ordinary country parson."

As the two detectives entered the Church of St. Blaise, David Walden began to play the music for the last hymn, and the choir burst into song. The response of the congregation, spread around the large building, sounded thin. As was to be expected, there were many more people present than there had been at Tobias Finner's funeral, but unlike on that occasion, they were not all clustered together in the front of the church.

Tansey and Greenway slipped into a rear pew and, to the chief inspector's surprise, his sergeant began to sing in a clear, pure soprano. They were standing by themselves, and suddenly he felt her hand holding tightly to his. As the hymn ended she released her grip.

"To the crypt for some lunch, sir?" she asked blandly, as people began to file out.

Lady Gerart greeted them at the bottom of the stone steps which led to the rapidly filling crypt.

"More than we expected," she said, "but I'm afraid many of them rarely come to church, and are only here today out of curiosity. On the other hand, some regular communicants made excuses because of the tragedy. Perhaps it's not quite the parish luncheon atmosphere we hoped for. It would have made Father Payne sad, I'm sure. Anyway, please do help yourselves to anything you like. There'll be plenty for everyone."

Trestle tables had been arranged at the sides of the crypt, between the stone arches, with willing helpers behind them. Small tables and chairs were scattered around. But most people were still standing, among them several known to Tansey and Greenway. Miss Mabson bowed to them. Veronica Gerart waved a greeting. Colonel Brevint nodded good morning and, to Tansey's amusement, steered his wife well away from them. Nor did David Walden show any desire to speak to them.

"In spite of Lady Gerart, I'm not sure we're all that welcome," said Tansey, finishing a mug of excellent soup. "Let's get some of that good-smelling chicken dish, and then circulate separately. You go and talk to Mrs. Dolbel; she could be a mine of information. I'll try Courtney."

"Yes, sir," said Greenway, "but here's Sir William."

"Chief Inspector, I've got some news for you," Sir William said. "As you know I've been talking to Bishop Payne. He can't get back from Africa before the end of next week, and I understand his wife's not too well—that's why she didn't accompany him on his trip. But the bishop's secretary is coming down to Oxford tomorrow. He'll be staying with us at the Manor for a day or two, but as soon as he arrives he'll go to see you at Kidlington. I took the liberty of giving him your name, and I told him I was sure you'd do anything you could for him."

"Of course, sir, but I—I do have other duties," said Tansey. "I have to attend the post-mortem on Mr. Payne tomorrow morning, and there will be an inquest later in the week, which will almost certainly be adjourned. Do the bishop's family and his secretary know the circumstances of Blaise Payne's death? And have they been in contact with Miss Payne, the sister?"

Sir William was a little nonplussed by these sudden questions. "I only spoke to the bishop on the phone, as you know, but I told him what I could," he said. "Naturally he was upset, so I didn't want to add to the shock by going into details. You know, Chief Inspector, I could almost wish it had been thieves trying to steal the damned church silver. At least it would have made everything seem much simpler. As it is . . ." He shook his head. "And I've left it to you to put the secretary in the picture. As for the sister, I gather they are trying to get in touch with her. She's said to be somewhere in the West Country." Sir William nodded, and walked away.

"Is she, by Jove?" said Tansey to Greenway. "I thought she was going back to London. Oh well, I expect we'll find her soon."

As they had agreed, Tansey and Greenway collected some food and went in search of their different targets. Mrs. Dolbel had nothing but praise for Father Payne, but she hadn't liked his sister, whom she described as something of a "hussy," who smoked and drank and didn't seem to care how few clothes she wore around the house, which wasn't decent, especially in front of a priest.

"To tell the truth, miss," she said, "I was glad when she left, though it was a bit sudden, like her arrival. But poor Father Payne! So sad to die like that. And so brave of him. I only hope you catch them what did it."

This seemed to be the general opinion. There was no overt criticism of Father Payne, and the story that he had died to save the silver from thieves appeared to be accepted. If some people found this slightly incredible or implausible, they kept their views to themselves on this occasion, which had taken on something of the character of a wake.

Even John Courtney was discreet until Tansey asked him directly why he had implied that the woman he had met in Oxford with Payne was not the parson's sister, as she claimed.

"I've rarely seen two people look less alike," he said, "though I know there's no guarantee that a brother and sister will resemble each other. But it wasn't just the lack of any resemblance." He glanced around to make sure they were not being overheard. "Between you and me, it was the way she kissed him that struck me, full on the lips—a long, lingering kiss, more like lovers than relations—and the fact that he was embarrassed when he saw me. Still, we're all human and the poor chap's dead now."

With a casual wave of his hand Courtney went off in search of more food, and Tansey found himself confronted by Tom Cresford, who said, "Remember me, sir? I'm the verger. You were at old Tobias Finner's funeral. I saw you by the side door when Father Payne just stopped those idiot pall-bearers from dropping the coffin. Complain like anything they did about it being that heavy, when poor Tobias can't have weighed more than a feather or two."

"Yes, of course I remember, Mr. Cresford," said Tansey. "This must be a sad day for you. I imagine you knew Mr. Payne better than most people."

"Not very well, sir. He'd not been here long, and he wasn't an easy man to get to know. But pleasant enough, mind, and ready to take advice about how things should be done. Those who killed him deserve to suffer."

"I suppose you haven't seen any strangers hanging around the cottage—or the church—recently, have you?" Tansey asked casually.

Cresford shook his head. "Suspicious-looking characters, you mean, sir? No. There was a party of Americans at the beginning of the week, and some kids from a school in Abingdon. Then there was a couple who came into the church yesterday afternoon, when it was closed to visitors. But Miss Mabson could tell you about them. She spoke to them."

Tansey thanked him, and went over to Miss Mabson, who was talking to Lady Gerart. He wasn't hopeful that she would be able to add anything to what Lady Gerart had already told him, and he made the effort more for something to do than for any other reason. He was thinking it was time for him and Hilary Greenway to get back to Kidlington.

"Of course I remember them," said Jane Mabson. "A pleasant couple. They didn't argue when I explained why the church was closed. It seemed to me that Father Payne was unduly shaken by their appearance, though I can't think why."

"I've mentioned the incident to the chief inspector, Jane," Lady Gerart said. Then to Tansey, "You—"

"Of course I remember," said Tansey thoughtfully. "It would be interesting to know more about that couple."

CHAPTER 16

Chief Inspector Tansey sat in the pathologist's office, drinking coffee. He had attended many post-mortems during his career, but he had never become accustomed to them. They stripped the man or woman on the slab of any human dignity that he or she might have possessed in life and, Tansey felt, should retain in death. Even the most derelict being had some quality worthy of respect, or at least of pity.

"—a fascinating body, especially for a parson." The more practical pathologist unknowingly interrupted these ruminations. "Those burn marks on his feet are understandable in the light of what you've told me. Someone wanted to get some information out of him—and probably succeeded."

"Why do you say that?"

"Because the burn marks form a pattern on the sole of the left foot—a pattern that's incomplete on the sole of the right foot. The logical conclusion is that the villain got what he wanted, unless he was disturbed."

Tansey nodded. "I hadn't thought of that. It fits the most likely theory about what happened. They—it's logical to think there were at least two of them, and a vague indication there were only two—they got what they were after and departed leaving Payne alive. It was Payne's bad luck they'd been careless with their cigarettes, and he was to die of smoke inhalation."

"Their bad luck, too, if you catch them."

"Yes. It'll be a murder charge—or more probably man-slaughter in the circumstances. But I can't see a British judge taking kindly to the idea of torture."

"Then there's the bullet wound in the chest—that's what really interests me, Dick," the pathologist continued. "A centimetre to the right and it would have killed him. And the date —I'd put it at approximately seven to ten years old. What was your Father Payne doing to get shot at a decade ago? He was never a padre in one of the services, was he?"

"I haven't a clue," Tansey admitted. "No one's mentioned him as a padre. I only hope Bishop Payne or his wife or his secretary can supply some answers." He frowned. "Are you sure the wound's as old as that?"

"Well, it certainly wasn't last year's vintage." Pathologists were incurably facetious, Tansey thought. "The scar tissue—" The telephone interrupted what he was about to say. He listened for a second and passed the receiver to Tansey. "For you. Sergeant Greenway."

"Hello, Sergeant," Tansey said.

"Sir, I've got Bishop Payne's secretary here at headquarters —a Mr. Derek Carter-Wood. He's prepared to identify the body, and he can do so right now, if you agree and if it's convenient. He would make any other necessary arrangements at the same time."

"Hang on," said Tansey, and covered the receiver. "Bishop Payne's secretary wants to view the body. Will it be OK—in reasonable order—in twenty minutes or so?"

"Why not? My assistant's tidying it up now, and anyway the chap will only want to see the face."

Tansey removed his hand from the mouthpiece. "That'll be all right, Sergeant, but warn him it may not be too pretty a sight—and that we shall probably want to interview the bishop himself as soon as he returns. And you come along here with this Carter-Wood man. On the way see what he knows about Payne. And see if they're any further ahead than we are with tracing the sister."

"I'll do my best, sir."

Twenty minutes later Sergeant Greenway and Mr. Carter-Wood were shown into the pathologist's office. Carter-Wood was in his late forties. A short, dark, studious-looking man, he was clearly businesslike, and had no desire to waste anyone's time. Greenway had already given him a somewhat more detailed account of how Payne had died than that provided by Sir William Gerart, and he asked at once to see the body.

"Then, perhaps, Chief Inspector, you'd fill in the picture for me," he said. "It's bad enough that Bishop Payne's nephew should die in an unfortunate accident, but the surrounding circumstances seem to be utterly incomprehensible. According to the car radio on the way down, Mr. Payne was protecting the silver of St. Blaise's Church from thieves, but I gather from your sergeant that this may not be the case."

He didn't wait for a response from Tansey, but followed the pathologist from the room. The chief inspector immediately glanced interrogatively at Greenway, who shook her head.

"Father Payne had a sister, all right, and she did have a nervous breakdown, during which the parson abandoned his job as a curate to look after her. She's now quite recovered and, as they said, is thought to be somewhere in Devon or Cornwall. Neither Mrs. Payne nor Carter-Wood have an address for her, and they're hoping we can trace her. And Carter-Wood also confirmed that Father Payne's previous appointment had been in the East End of London. He made one odd remark—'Heaven knows what he got up to in the big city'—but I couldn't get him to amplify that statement."

Tansey laughed. "He may find he has to, and under oath," he said. "Any news of Payne's dubious friends?"

"You mean the couple who came into the church on Saturday afternoon? They were seen walking through the village. They could easily have left a motorbike behind a hedge outside the place, but there's really nothing to connect them with the two seen on a bike by that young boy later on."

"True, but it's interesting that Payne may have been overcome at the sight of the pair in the church," Tansey remarked. "I'm sure we can rely on Lady Gerart's account of the incident, and I'm prepared to bet that if we can trace that couple we'll find out a whole lot more than we know at present." He paused. "Now we'd better go and witness the identification. Do you want to come?"

They were forestalled before Greenway could answer. The office door opened suddenly and Mr. Carter-Wood almost stumbled into the room, followed by the pathologist, who went straight to the washbasin in a corner and produced a glass of water. The bishop's secretary was very pale, and there were beads of sweat on his upper lip. He sat down heavily, took out a handkerchief and mopped his face as he sipped at the water.

"I had to show him the whole body, not just the face," the pathologist said, "so that he could be sure."

Tansey was about to ask, "Sure of what?" when Carter-Wood swallowed hard and declared, "And I am absolutely sure, Chief Inspector. I would swear it on the Bible—and so would the bishop. That man is not Blaise Payne, Bishop Payne's nephew."

"What?"

Nothing that Carter-Wood might have said could have surprised Tansey and Greenway more. They stared at him as if he were out of his mind, but he reiterated his statement.

"I know Blaise Payne well. I've known him for years. He's the same build as that chap, and not unlike him. But Blaise is not so dark, nor so hirsute. Blaise's eyes are hazel, not brown, and he certainly hasn't got that bullet wound. I've seen him stripped often enough when we've been swimming. You must believe me."

"We do believe you, of course, Mr. Carter-Wood," said Tansey. "But this is something of a shock. How it came about I haven't the faintest idea, but, as you know, that dead man whom you've just seen has been masquerading as the Reverend Blaise Payne in Fairfield for the last several weeks."

"It's going to be a shock to Bishop Payne too," said Carter-Wood, who had by now recovered much of his composure, "and, I suppose, to the Gerarts and innumerable other people. It's—it's hard to credit."

"And it raises some interesting questions," said Tansey. "If the dead man's not Blaise Payne, then who the hell is he? He arrived in Fairfield on the day he was expected. He appears to have known exactly where to go. He's got Payne's clothes and books and possessions, and he's been able to play the role of a parson without creating any suspicions."

Carter-Wood was quick on the uptake. "Chief Inspector, you're suggesting there was some kind of conspiracy between Blaise Payne and this dead man?"

"It's not beyond the bounds of possibility, is it?"

"No-o, perhaps not." Carter-Wood wasn't going to commit himself. "But I had a long talk with Blaise when the idea was mooted that, subject to everyone's agreement, he might come to Fairfield as a priest-in-charge—almost as an experiment. I would have sworn he was anxious to try the life of a parson in a country living." He sighed, then asked suddenly, "On the other hand, where is he?"

Carter-Wood had spoken with conviction and sincerity, and for a minute there was silence. The bishop's secretary had no idea what was in the minds of the others; there was no reason why he should. He lived in the North of England and, though he heard and watched the general news, and read *The Times* and the *Telegraph*, a body found in Copley Wood, even if he'd noticed any reference to it, would mean nothing to him. There were murders, rapes, innumerable serious crimes committed every day.

Tansey said heavily, "Mr. Carter-Wood, you've already had one troublesome experience today, and a considerable shock. Nevertheless, I'm afraid I must ask you to view another body. I fear there's a strong chance that this one may really be that of Blaise Payne."

"Another body?" demanded Carter-Wood. "Also killed in that fire at Church Cottage?"

Tansey shook his head. "No, it was found in a shallow grave in Copley Wood, which is not very far from Fairfield. A silver button was lying nearby, suggesting some connection with an Oxford social club, to which we know that Mr. Payne belonged."

"And you think—"

"Let's first make sure it's not another stranger, Mr. Carter-Wood. While we believed that Mr. Payne was alive and well and performing his duties, it never occurred to me that there might have been a substitution, but—"

"And why on earth should you have thought of it?" the pathologist asked.

"Why, indeed?" said Tansey. "I only hope my chief constable will take the same view, and agree that he couldn't expect such brilliance on anyone's part." He stood up. "Mr. Carter-Wood, it'll mean a short drive to another mortuary—do you mind?"

"No, of course not." Carter-Wood pushed back his chair. "I'm ready. I was just wondering if I should try to contact Bishop Payne again. But it would be difficult. And, as you say, let's make sure first. Dear God, I can't imagine what the bishop will say about all this."

After further intercontinental telephone calls, Bishop Payne cut short his pastoral visit and flew back from Africa overnight. He appeared in Oxford, and confirmed Carter-Wood's statement—that the body from the burning house was not that of his nephew. He seemed stunned, as were the Gerarts, David Walden and Jane Mabson—though all for somewhat different reasons. To the bishop, now staying with the Gerarts at Fairfield Manor, it seemed as if his nephew, of whom he had been very fond, had died twice. He had been trying to absorb the knowledge that the young man had probably been left to die a horrible death by criminals with whom he might once have been associated. Now he had to readjust his thoughts and accept that the man for whom he had been feeling love and pity was almost certainly his nephew's murderer.

But he had never met the false parson personally. Unlike

the others, he hadn't shaken his hand, consulted him on church affairs, entertained him to dinner, accepted his blessing, even received communion from him—or, in the case of David Walden, risked his own life in an attempt to save him. Admittedly the man had been in Fairfield only a few weeks, but as priest-in-charge he had been in a position to make a vastly greater impact in the community than any ordinary new resident.

Tansey sympathized with all the people gathered in the drawing-room of the Manor, and especially with those who had accepted without question the man they had believed to be Father Payne. He knew they must feel themselves deceived, betrayed, almost despoiled, and the last thing they wanted was to be reminded of the facts. But he had a job to do.

"Sir," he said, turning to Bishop Payne, "I know it's a subjective question, but what sort of man was your nephew? Was he an extrovert? Would he have picked up a hitch-hiker on a long drive—a complete stranger—and talked freely to him?"

The bishop considered the question seriously before he answered. "Yes," he said finally. "He was a friendly, outgoing person. He would probably have picked up a single man without thinking twice about it. And I dare say he'd have been happy to talk while they were travelling together. He was a trusting man, too trusting for his own good, seemingly."

"I see, sir," said Tansey thoughtfully. "Do you think he could have been acquainted with the man who took his place?"

"It's conceivable, I suppose," said the bishop. "But surely the chances that a man he knew was standing by the side of the road at a particular time on a particular day waiting for him were pretty remote. Unless—"

The bishop paused and thought for a moment, glancing at Mr. Carter-Wood. "I see what you meant when you suggested the possibility of conspiracy to Derek here."

At this point Sir William Gerart, who had been growing increasingly impatient, took it upon himself to intervene. "Instead of interrogating Bishop Payne about his nephew at a time like this, wouldn't it be more use if you were to try and discover who this impostor was, Chief Inspector?"

"Others are doing that, Sir William, I assure you," said Tansey, "and all these points could be of the utmost importance."

Sir William subsided as the bishop sighed. "As I said, I understand the implications of your question, Chief Inspector. But don't get a wrong impression. I suppose some of his colleagues might claim that my nephew was sometimes a little gullible, perhaps. But I refuse to believe that he was ever involved in any activity that could remotely be called criminal."

"I see. Thank you, sir." Tansey then turned to Lady Gerart and Miss Mabson. "You were the first to greet the man you supposed was Father Payne on his arrival in Fairfield. Would you tell me exactly what happened?"

"First, he was late," Jane Mabson said bluntly. "Lady Gerart and I were waiting for him at Church Cottage, and we were thinking of giving him up and leaving when he eventually appeared. He'd lost his way, and he'd also killed a—a cat, or so he said. He was upset about it."

"A cat?" said Tansey, remembering the old photograph he had found at Church Cottage, among the pseudo-priest's possessions.

He turned to Bishop Payne. "Sir," he asked, "did your nephew have a cat years ago, perhaps when he was a child, called—called—?" He looked at Sergeant Greenway.

"Blodge, sir."

"Blodge," repeated Tansey to the bishop.

"No," said the bishop. "Blaise never had a pet. It was an odd quirk of his, but he disliked cats, dogs—all animals, in fact. Is that important?"

Tansey didn't explain about the photograph. "Probably not, sir," he said, and continued with his questions.

"Now, sir," he said to Bishop Payne, "let's turn to Blaise's sister, your niece, whom we're all trying to find. I take it her name wasn't Kay?"

"Indeed not, Chief Inspector. She's called Edith. An old-fashioned name, perhaps, for a modern young girl, but still . . ."

"Yes, sir. Now you'll understand why the next point is crucial. Does Miss Edith Payne have red hair?"

"Good heavens, no!" said the bishop. "She's a blonde and a very attractive one." He paused for a moment. "And I'm quite sure she wouldn't dye it red."

"Just as I thought," said Tansey, as the rest of those present drew breath. He had more questions to ask, as he tried to create from the various impressions of these people a valid picture of the man who had so successfully impersonated the Reverend Blaise Payne, and the woman who had claimed to be his sister.

"What a day!" said Tansey as Greenway drove him back to Kidlington. "And all we've achieved is to substitute one dead mystery man for another. We now know pretty well all we need to know about the corpse from Copley Wood, but practically nothing about his impersonator."

"We do have a few facts, sir. He was a well-educated man, with a knowledge of religious procedures and the duties of a Church of England parson. He must have been a good actor, too, to be able to play the part, unless—"

"Unless—" Tansey prompted.

"I was wondering if he could have been a parson once himself. Then something went wrong and . . ." Greenway left her sentence unfinished.

"He was unfrocked," Tansey suggested. "So we have an unfrocked parson, with an old gunshot wound, who loved cats—especially one called Blodge—and had a red-haired girlfriend and possibly a violent temper which caused him to kill when it suited him. A wonderful picture, Sergeant."

But, strangely enough, it was not so very far from the truth.

CHAPTER 17

"William Crowe Denville!"

Tansey's triumphant cry greeted Greenway as she entered the chief inspector's office about ten o'clock on Tuesday morning. She had been given a couple of hours' leave for a dental appointment, and thus was a good deal later than usual. She gave the chief inspector a puzzled frown. The name Denville meant nothing to her, but it was clearly of considerable importance.

"I'm sorry, sir, but—"

"That is the name of the man who impersonated Father Payne—William Crowe Denville. Billy Denville. The Met identified him from his prints overnight."

"I thought that might be what you meant, sir, but still—"

"You've never heard of Billy Denville? That's almost like saying you've never heard of Wild Bill Hickok. But admittedly the Denville case was some years ago—before you joined the force, Sergeant. Nevertheless, it was one of the biggest crimes of the decade, at least in terms of the amount they got away with."

"You mean he—they—robbed a bank?"

"No, not a bank," said Tansey. "A jeweller's in Hatton Garden. It was uncut diamonds—uncut large and fine gemstones —that were stolen. Their value was estimated at a million and a half sterling—and that was ten years ago, as I say. If I remember rightly there was a reward of nearly ten percent—a hundred thousand pounds—offered for information leading to the conviction of the thieves and the return of the loot. I don't know if it's still available. Certainly the diamonds have never been recovered."

"A pity that police officers can't accept rewards," said Greenway.

Tansey laughed. "You mean we could retire to a Caribbean island together?" Hilary Greenway looked up in surprise. Dick Tansey rarely made such remarks when they were on duty.

"Yes, sir," she said, taking care not to grin.

"There were three of them, plus Denville, in the gang," Tansey continued, "a man and two women. They were all young, in their twenties, and none of them had any kind of conviction or record. The robbery was planned meticulously, supposedly by Billy Denville, and might have succeeded except for some unlucky chance. It was a tunnelling job, and I think a water main burst and cut off their escape route. Anyway, three of them got caught, but Billy escaped temporarily."

"With the diamonds?" Greenway was fascinated.

"The others said yes. Billy claimed no. The judge believed them rather than Billy, for two reasons. The three didn't put up any resistance and they were captured on the site, as it were. None of them had an opportunity to get rid of the stuff or pass it to anyone. Billy, on the other hand, was free for several days before he was picked up down in the East End of London—"

"And—" said Greenway.

"This was a tricky point, and caused a lot of poor publicity for the Met. Billy Denville wasn't armed, but the police thought he was and he got shot. Hence the bullet wound, from which he damned near died."

"And the diamonds?"

"Well, the Met and everyone else took part in a hell of a search for them. Billy was put under a lot of pressure—I wouldn't be surprised if they offered him a trade-off—but he gave nothing away. Subsequently he was given a ten-year stretch, of which he served seven. He was released three months ago, having been a model prisoner, and still swearing he had no idea what happened to the diamonds."

"And the other three?"

"They got shorter sentences. Kay Turner, Billy's girlfriend, only served a few months in the end. But both his accomplices and the authorities were prepared to wait for Billy to come out. I can assure you that the police, as well as the insurance investigators, were all set to keep a pretty strict eye on him when he was released—and on the rest of the gang. What actually happened was that someone slipped up, and Billy was let out a few days earlier than was planned. The prison authorities hadn't let anyone know, so Billy had a chance to disappear—and he took it."

There was a slight pause before Tansey went on, "The Met were most annoyed—and so was everyone else involved, I suppose—but there wasn't much anyone could do. A nation-wide hunt came to nothing. They tried to keep tabs on the other three for a while, in the hope they might lead them to Billy—but no luck. So they gave that up after three months or so."

"Three months is a long time to manage to stay under cover," said Greenway.

"Oh, there's no doubt that Billy was a pretty smart operator in some ways. In fact, the next person we know of who set eyes on him was the real Blaise Payne, when Billy was hitch-hiking on the road to Oxford."

"And Billy got into conversation with Payne, and decided to impersonate him—a parson. It seems an odd choice."

"Not quite so odd, perhaps. I'll explain in a minute. Anyway, we've got as far as this: Blaise Payne unluckily offered Billy Denville a lift; Payne talked too much, and put the idea of impersonation into Denville's head."

"He must have been crazy to think he could get away with it for long. Sooner or later he'd be bound to bump into someone who knew Payne. Wasn't his uncle the bishop meant to be visiting the Gerarts later in the year, for example? And that barrister friend of Simon Ashe? In any case I don't understand how Billy Denville was able to impersonate a clergyman with such success, among knowledgeable people like Miss Mabson and Lady Gerart."

"I doubt if Billy intended to keep it up for long, and the mechanics were quite simple. He had all Payne's clothes and papers. Initially he didn't even have to bother to forge Payne's signature with any accuracy; his cut and bandaged hand took care of any questions from a bank manager who'd never met him. And he could have had a motive for wanting to stick around near Oxford for a week or so. But his ex-girlfriend Kay found him—and there could have been more than chance involved in that, too—and presumably told the rest of the gang where he was."

"And his knowledge of—what shall I call it—the religious routine? He can't have learnt all that from Blaise Payne during a hitch-hike."

"Ah," said Tansey. "That's one important point. What you don't know is that Billy Denville was brought up in a rectory. His father was a clergyman, and he was brought up in the right atmosphere, as it were."

"I see," said Greenway. "And—"

"And it may also have been his motive for wanting to be around here. His father retired just about the time that Billy was arrested, and came to live near Abingdon—not very far away. It's a long shot, but it represents a possible reason for Billy's need to visit this area, once he'd given the authorities and the rest of his gang the slip—"

"You mean the diamonds may be in his father's house. But surely at the time years ago the place must have been turned over with a fine-tooth comb."

"It certainly was, Sergeant, and his father must have been aware of the kind of life his son was living, because at first he swore he had no son, then finally admitted he hadn't seen him for years. As I said, it's a long shot, but the fact that Billy came back to a place nearby may indicate something, don't you think? And, as I also hinted earlier, it could be the reason for the woman Kay being in Oxford too."

"So the theory is that Kay, having guessed he might come in this direction, found him in Cornmarket Street, told his so-called friends, and then they forced him to say what he'd done with the diamonds. As you say, there's a lot to prove."

"True enough, but . . ." Tansey was thoughtful. "We'll have to wait until we catch Kay Turner and his other erstwhile friends. At least we know who we're looking for—they're a brother and sister called Ron and Sandra Wilson—and a real brother and sister this time. It shouldn't be too difficult to track them down, not with their records and every police officer in the country on the alert. The fugitives will know about the fire and Billy's death by now, so whatever plans they might have made will have been upset and they'll be running scared."

"Presumably, if there's anything in your idea about the location of the diamonds, they'll be running in the direction of Father's house. Surely we've got the place under surveillance, sir. The old man may be in danger."

"Give us a chance, Sergeant Greenway. We only established Billy Denville's identity a few hours ago. And a report's just come in. Naturally, once we knew it was Billy, the local Abingdon station was asked to inform the father of his death. It turns out that the old clergyman has been in hospital for over a week, after a minor operation. He's due to be discharged tomorrow. His reaction was the same as years ago—he swore he had no son, had never had a son. In the circumstances, the locals are taking no further action, except to keep his house under observation. We'll be seeing the old man ourselves later —tomorrow, when he's out of hospital—though I've got grave doubts whether an interview will get us any further forward."

"Very good, sir," said Sergeant Greenway.

"In the meantime, a treasure hunt to find the diamonds isn't our only job. Blaise Payne's real sister has been traced— in the West Country, as was suggested—and she's on her way to Oxford. I can't see how we're going to get anything new out of her, but as a matter of form if she's been the subject of an impersonation we should see her."

"Yes, sir," said Sergeant Greenway.

"But first of all I shall want us to pay another visit to Fairfield this afternoon, and encourage the officers searching Church Cottage to look for clues about Denville as well as the diamonds, and perhaps talk to one or two more people who can provide confirmatory evidence."

"Yes, sir," said Greenway. "Do you want me to try and make appointments?"

"With Miss Mabson, perhaps," Tansey said. "Let's take her first, before we go to the cottage. The rest we'll leave to chance. Most of them should be at home on a day like this."

It was a bitterly cold afternoon. The snow had melted, but there were icy patches on the road, and Hilary Greenway drove carefully. By now the route to Fairfield was so familiar to her that she didn't have to think about it, and she let her mind wander. Billy Denville was not the first murderer she had come across, but he intrigued her as a character.

Tansey had been busy that morning. Nevertheless, he had taken time to put her fairly fully in the picture about Billy's background, which was more than many senior officers would have bothered to do. She knew why this was so, but she had never tried to take advantage of their special off-duty relationship. Somehow it was different now, driving through the Oxfordshire countryside in the warm intimacy of the car.

"What about Billy's mother?" she asked suddenly.

"She walked out on her husband when Billy was a child. Maybe that helped to sour Billy's father." Tansey shrugged. "But don't get sentimental about Billy, Sergeant Greenway. Lots of people have had vastly worse starts in life, and haven't ended up as criminals or murderers."

"Of course," said Greenway. "And I'm not getting sentimental about him. But you must admit it would be interesting to know exactly how William Crowe Denville progressed through his disturbed life till he became a killer."

Tansey grinned. He knew she was right. To understand how people worked, to be able to put yourself in the place of the

villain, often meant the difference between success and fail-
ure in a case. And you needed to put yourself in the victim's
place, too. If Blaise Payne had been a different kind of
man . . .

"Sergeant, you've got me philosophizing now," Tansey said,
"but we'd better be practical. Here we are at The Hall."

The Hall, which had been in Miss Mabson's family for
many years, was almost as imposing as the Manor. It was a
fine house, built of Cotswold stone, with extensive grounds,
and much too large for one middle-aged lady. A stout, elderly
maid showed them into a booklined room which had a pleasant view over the hills.

Miss Mabson appeared almost at once. She greeted them
and offered them coffee. When Tansey refused, she waved
them to chairs which would have looked at home in a London
club. Greenway sat, but Tansey stayed on his feet.

"Miss Mabson, would you be kind enough to study these
carefully, and tell me if you recognize any of the subjects?"

Jane Mabson took the file of photographs that Tansey
handed to her, and began to sift through them. Almost at once
she exclaimed, "But of course, this is Father Payne—" She
stopped and sighed. "I find it extremely hard not to think of
that wicked man as Father Payne," she said.

"His real name is Denville," said Tansey.

Miss Mabson nodded. "And this is the young woman who
was supposed to be his sister." She passed Tansey a photograph of Kay. "She's unmistakable. A thoroughly unpleasant
character, as I believe I told you, Chief Inspector. Indeed,
when Lady Gerart asked me to have dinner with them the
Saturday before last and I understood she was to be present, I
felt I must decline. Fortunately for me, she decided to go to
London, so I was able to accept."

"So she left Fairfield more than a week before the fire at
Church Cottage?" said Tansey.

"That's right. She left the Saturday of that dinner party I
mentioned. Father P.—that man—took her into Oxford to
catch a London train, and he had trouble with his car and was

late arriving at the Manor. At least—" Miss Mabson eyed the police officers shrewdly and paused. "That's what he told us, Chief Inspector. It could have been a lie, I suppose, like so much else. She could have gone anywhere."

"We hope to catch up with her soon, Miss Mabson," said Tansey. "As you can imagine, she has a lot of questions to answer." He took back the photographs, and Sergeant Greenway produced another file. "What about these? Do you recognize anyone among this lot?"

This time Jane Mabson was much slower in reacting. She sorted twice through the prints before she chose two. "I think," she said slowly, "that these are the couple who came into St. Blaise's Church on the day before the fire, when we were getting ready for the feast. But I couldn't swear to it, Chief Inspector. They look younger here, and their hair is quite different."

"Thank you," said Tansey, taking back the photographs. The two photographs Miss Mabson had picked were those of Billy Denville's remaining accomplices. "We're most grateful."

"I wish I could be sure," said Miss Mabson, frowning. "If I could see them and perhaps speak to them— Are they the two who caused the fire?"

"We think it's a good possibility," admitted Tansey.

From The Hall, Greenway drove the chief inspector through Fairfield village to the Church of St. Blaise. The lane to the cottage and the surrounding area had once again been cordoned off, and the incident van was back in place, together with a mass of other official vehicles and a crowd of police officers, both uniformed and in plain clothes. A uniformed officer saluted and let them through, and they found an Inspector Colman waiting for them. He took them out of the cold into the hall of the cottage. Sounds of rending and banging drifted down from upstairs.

"Nothing so far inside the building, sir," he said, "but they're practically taking the place apart, as you can hear. If there are any diamonds to be found, we'll find them."

"It's only an outside chance," said Tansey, "but it would be a pity to miss them if they did happen to be here."

There was an excited shout from outside, hurried steps, and a loud knock at the door. The inspector answered it and muttered to a uniformed sergeant. Tansey, whose hearing was acute, caught the words "boot" and "bag," but didn't immediately associate them.

"Sir." Colman turned to him. "The old car in the garage is being searched. The boot had to be forced open, and there's a fairly large bit of luggage—a suitcase—inside, the kind you'd take for a long weekend, perhaps. It's locked and strapped. It looks as if our man might have been contemplating a quick departure."

"But he left a lot of his clothes, some of them new, in the cupboard, sir," Greenway protested.

"Maybe he had others, Sergeant. Anyway, I'm having the bag photographed *in situ*, then fingerprinted." The inspector turned to Tansey. "Would you like it opened where it is, sir, or brought in here?"

"Call us when you're ready to open it," Tansey said. "Meantime, I'll go upstairs and give the officers working there a word of encouragement."

"Very good, sir. We shan't be long," said Colman.

Indeed, it was only a few minutes before he reappeared in Church Cottage to say that the suitcase was ready to be opened. The inspector removed the strap himself and, fiddling with a penknife, easily forced the locks. The case, which was over-full, at once sprang open of its own accord, revealing a collection of clothes.

"Photographs," said Tansey at once. Then, as the bulbs flashed, he carefully, and with a certain distaste, fingered through the contents, trying to cause a minimum of disturbance. The clothing obviously belonged to a woman. There was also a make-up kit and a brush and comb. Several red hairs still adhered to the brush. He pointed to them.

"Kay Turner, sir?" said Greenway.

"It seems likely," Tansey agreed. "Here's a coat and make-up, and a handbag and, as the inspector said, what you'd expect to take away for a long weekend. But why is all this here in Fairfield? Kay Turner's meant to have gone to London last Saturday, according to Miss Mabson and the others."

"She wouldn't have gone without her luggage." Colman stated the obvious. "Let's hope she hasn't ended up in Copley Wood, sir."

"How right you are," said Tansey. "We're already looking for her, of course, but this is going to mean more work. Seeing that we're here, Inspector, Sergeant Greenway and I will make a few inquiries. Will you get the bag to Forensic in Kidlington?" He added some more instructions, and said to Greenway, "Let's go and talk to Mrs. Dolbel."

Mrs. Dolbel, however, was not at home. No amount of knocking at her front door produced a response. But a passing nighbour stopped.

"If it's Mrs. Dolbel you're looking for," she said, "you'll find her at the old vicarage. It's one of her days for the Brevints, is Tuesday. But she should be back soon."

"Damn!" said Tansey as they got into the car. "I want her alone."

"And you're in luck, sir," said Greenway, who had been adjusting the rear-view mirror and seen Mrs. Dolbel hurrying along the street. "Here she comes."

Tansey jumped out of the car and caught Mrs. Dolbel as she was putting the key in the lock of her door.

"Oh dear," she said. "Is it more questions? I've told the police all I know about—about him—and I'm that upset. To think I cooked his meals and washed his clothes and even bandaged his hand when he cut it. I—I simply can't believe it all."

"Actually we'd like to talk to you about the girl he called his sister. Her name is Kay Turner."

"I wondered about that, I must say," said Mrs. Dolbel, letting them through the front door, and showing them into the little front parlour, which looked as if it were rarely used. "I mean about her being his sister or not. Somehow she didn't always behave like a sister."

Tansey let Mrs. Dolbel talk. She told them of Kay's unexpected arrival, and her smoking and drinking. She mentioned how Kay had obviously shocked Miss Mabson by appearing "in one of those negligée things," when Miss Mabson had come to talk about Tobias Finner's funeral.

"—and that was the last day I saw Miss Payne, as she called herself—that Wednesday. Because of the funeral I wasn't at Church Cottage much on Friday, and she wasn't well. He said she was spending the day in bed and wasn't to be disturbed. Actually I did knock at her door, but there wasn't any answer. I even tried the door, thinking she might need something, but she'd locked it. And I didn't see her on the Saturday morning when I popped in with some laundry I'd done for her. He said he was driving her into Oxford to catch a train to London because she'd suddenly decided to leave."

"So," said Tansey as he and Greenway were returning to Kidlington, "Kay was alive and well on Wednesday afternoon, but said to be ill on Friday and to have left for London on Saturday—but evidently without her luggage. Of course, there may be a simple explanation—time and a hell of a lot of checking will tell—but I'm very much afraid we've got another murder on our hands."

CHAPTER 18

By lunch-time the next day—Wednesday—Tansey had no doubt that Kay Turner had been killed by Billy Denville. It turned out that Mrs. Dolbel had not been the last person to see her alive. Kay had been sighted on the Thursday of the week before St. Blaise's Feast Day, first by the postman, then by Tom Cresford the verger, and then by Sylvia Ashe, who had called at Church Cottage during the afternoon with some query about St. Blaise's choir. But Kay Turner had not been seen since that afternoon.

And, most importantly, no evidence could be found to show that a woman answering her description had taken any train —or bus—from Oxford on the Saturday when she was supposed to have left for London. It was conceivable that she had been given a lift, but in any case the presence of her suitcase, including all her personal possessions and especially her handbag, remained inexplicable.

Church Cottage was being searched yet again, this time for any signs of bloodstains or a possible murder weapon. Every single kitchen knife had been examined, for instance, and sent to the forensic science laboratory, but without result— except for a typically facetious phone report from one of the scientists that the carving knife had been used to cut up an animal, either lamb or beef. No traces of any other significance had yet been found, and Tansey expected none. Denville, after all, had been a strong man who would have had no difficulty in killing a petite girl like Kay with his bare hands.

The snow had melted, and the cottage garden and the nearby fields were being gone over, but this exercise was also proving fruitless. There were no indications of an attempt to dig anywhere. If Denville had indeed murdered his ex-girlfriend there was no clue as to what he had done with her body.

Inquiries were continuing about Kay Turner, naturally, on the off-chance that she was still alive, and about Ron and Sandra Wilson, the brother and sister who had completed the original gang, and whom Miss Mabson had identified with fair certainty as the couple she had met in St. Blaise's Church on the Saturday of the fire. But, in spite of a country-wide search, they too had apparently disappeared again. It was the opinion of the police that, scared by Billy Denville's death, for which they could be held responsible, Ron and Sandra had picked up the diamonds from wherever Denville had stashed them and gone to ground. But sooner or later they would presumably have to emerge, and the authorities would be ready. Or so the authorities hoped.

Tansey was not idle. He was fully occupied with the co-ordination of these multi-faceted investigations, but his work was interrupted by a sudden phone call from Abingdon. The Reverend Edward Denville had been discharged from hospital that morning, and on his return home had immediately demanded the presence of the police. His attitude to them had changed completely. The day before, seen in hospital, it had been one of total non-cooperation. Today however he was eager for their help.

Mr. Denville normally lived alone in a small house on the outskirts of Abingdon, and as soon as he had opened his front door he had staggered back in horror and anger.

His house had been burgled, apparently ransacked. Drawers had been pulled out and the contents strewn over the floor. Clothes had been emptied from cupboards and wardrobes, books thrown from shelves and the papers in his desk left in hopeless confusion. A small escritoire had been forced open. Rugs had been rolled up. And the kitchen was now littered with broken china, tins of food and dry goods. Even the bathroom hadn't escaped. The cover had been removed from the lavatory cistern, and towels, linen and toilet papers, normally kept in the airing cupboard, thrown into the bath.

Because poor eyesight prevented him from driving, Mr. Denville no longer kept a car. However, there was a garage attached to the house, and this too had been plundered. A pile of logs had been knocked over, and an old trunk full of books had been emptied and turned upside down.

Nevertheless, when questioned, Mr. Denville had to admit that nothing had been stolen. The little silver that he possessed had not been touched. A few pounds and some change, kept in a jar in the kitchen, remained intact. The television set, the video recorder and a fair selection of cassettes were still there.

"Vandals," Mr. Denville insisted. "It must have been vandals. No one else would commit such a crime. I could understand someone breaking in and stealing television equipment or the money, but this—this is pointless."

When he received this news, however, Tansey was not so sure. Whether or not the old parson chose to deny it, he was Billy Denville's father. Billy had died in the early hours of Sunday morning in violent circumstances. The Reverend Edward Denville's house was ransacked sometime later than the Saturday afternoon, when a friend and neighbour had come into the house to air the rooms, but earlier than today, Wednesday, when Denville himself had returned. It could be coincidence, but it looked very much as if—

Tansey lifted his phone. "Sergeant," he said, "get the car. We're off to Abingdon immediately."

On the doorstep, the chief inspector introduced himself and his companion to the old man. In spite of his earlier appeals for help to the local police, the parson was not welcoming to the officers from headquarters. He looked tired and grim, and only grudgingly agreed to see them, reluctantly showing them into his sitting-room, which had been restored to some sort of order, though the papers on the desk were in disarray and books were still on the floor.

Tansey had been wondering how to tackle this odd situation. At last, after the polite preliminaries, he asked gently, "When did you last see your son William, often known as Billy, Mr. Denville?"

"I have no son, Chief Inspector."

In the face of this outright denial, the chief inspector had no alternative but to change his tactics. "No, Mr. Denville," he said brutally. "You're quite right. You don't have a son any more. You've already been informed that he died in suspicious circumstances last Saturday night. I'm talking about William Crowe Denville, as you know very well, and this is a serious matter. You realize you could be arrested for obstructing the police in the course of their duties."

There was a long silence while the Reverend Edward Denville was clearly considering his position. At last he said, "I have not seen William for ages—not since he disgraced me by becoming a common thief. I got him a good solicitor and an expensive barrister, because I believed it was my duty, but when I discovered the enormity of his crime I wanted nothing more to do with him."

"You didn't see him immediately before he was apprehended by the police?"

"No, why should I? He'd left home years before that, and he never came to visit me. He never cared about me. He never cared about anyone or anything."

"Except Blodge," put in Greenway softly.

"Blodge? Ah yes, that wretched cat of his." Denville had caught the sergeant's remark. "Once when I beat the cat because it had made a mess on the carpet William attacked me with a cricket bat. Luckily he was only a boy then and I got it away from him easily. But he had always had a violent temper, and I suspect he'd have killed me if he could."

"Did he ever write to you—or send you a packet to keep for him?" Tansey asked.

The old man still had his wits about him. "Those diamonds, you mean? No, most certainly not." The parson laughed harshly. "And if he had I would immediately have turned them over to the appropriate authorities."

"So you had no correspondence with your son at all?"

There was a slight hesitation before Denville said bleakly, "Every year on his birthday he sent me a card, always with the same message: 'To remind you that I hate you.' At least I shan't get any more of those."

Good news awaited the chief inspector on his return to Kidlington. Sandra Wilson had been spotted in Reading by a bright police officer, just as she had come out of a supermarket with some shopping. The officer had radioed for help, and followed her to the house where she and her brother were lodging. Arresting them had been no problem; they were on their way to Oxford with a police escort, and should arrive within the hour.

"They can wait," said Tansey to the duty officer. "I'm going home to have a meal." He didn't add that Hilary Greenway would be going with him. "I'll be back later this evening. Make sure to keep the Wilsons separate when they arrive. They'll already have agreed on their story, but it might make them nervous to be allowed to stew alone for a while."

By 9:00 P.M. Tansey and Greenway had returned to headquarters. Ron Wilson was brought, very formally, to an interrogation room by a uniformed officer, who remained standing by the door. Tansey motioned to Wilson to sit across the bare table from him. Greenway was in a chair to one side, notebook open on her knee.

Tansey gave Wilson the official warning, and said, "Now, Mr. Wilson—"

"What am I charged with?"

"That can come later, if necessary. At the moment you and your sister are merely helping us with our inquiries."

Wilson's smile was cynical. He was in his early thirties, but looked younger. He was tow-haired with a pleasant face and a civilized manner. He modelled his appearance on a typical American college kid. In fact, he had been a petty criminal with aspirations until his sister, who was by far the stronger character, had managed to get them involved with Billy Denville and the Hatton Garden diamond robbery.

"But if you're interested right now," Tansey went on cheerfully, "the charges could include breaking and entering, larceny, committing grievous bodily harm, arson—and murder. You'd be an old man by the time you got out, Wilson."

Ron Wilson did not seem immediately perturbed. He gave a jeering laugh. "You must be joking, Inspector. You've got nothing on me, nor on Sandra. We made a mistake once, and we paid for it. Try and pin Billy Denville's death on us, and you'll be surprised how much support we get in the media. Here we are, doing our best to go straight, and you jump us. You've got no evidence—no proof."

Tansey was only too clearly aware that this was the truth. Jane Mabson would probably identify the Wilsons as the couple who had entered St. Blaise's Church on the Saturday of the fire in spite of a notice on the door, but there was nothing dramatically illegal about that. Constance Gerart would say that Billy Denville—Father Payne, as she knew him—had pleaded chest pains, apparently when he saw them, but that bit of evidence was pretty meaningless. There was a motive, certainly—the diamonds. The rest was surmise. The chief constable would never agree that the case should be put up to the DPP, because it was self-evident that he would throw it out.

Tansey decided to take a chance. He smiled. "You underrate me, Wilson—and the scientific resources of the Thames Valley Police. It's difficult to light cigarettes with gloves on, isn't it? And remember what saliva tests on the butts you left behind will show."

Tansey paused to see what effect these statements were having and was immediately rewarded. Ron Wilson was staring at him, frowning, doubtful. Slowly he licked his lips, thinking of saliva. His body was taut, and Tansey pressed home his advantage.

"You also miscalculated over Kay Turner. She wanted her share of the diamond money, and she didn't mind Billy getting a knock or two, but she was fond of him in her way. She didn't want him killed, and she most certainly doesn't want to be a partner to a conspiracy to murder. She'd rather shop you and Sandra any day."

"The bitch! The bitch!"

The exclamation was involuntary. Tansey kept his face free from expression. From the reports he had read on Ron Wilson he hadn't expected him to be particularly intelligent, but the breakthrough had come more quickly than he had hoped. However, the chief inspector knew he must handle the situation with great care; a mistake on his part now could ruin everything.

Wilson was breathing heavily. "She's turned Queen's evidence, has she?" he said at last. "I knew the bitch couldn't be trusted."

"What did you expect?" Tansey asked very carefully.

"But she doesn't know anything. She wasn't there. Whatever she told you, it's a lie. We didn't leave Billy to die. It was an accident. We didn't mean to kill him. Why should we when he'd told us—"

"Where he'd hidden the diamonds?" Tansey shook his head sadly. "You poor Wilsons! I'm sorry for you. Billy tricked you, didn't he? He sent you on a wild goose chase to his father's house, knowing you'd find nothing there—and incidentally he didn't give a damn what you might do to his father or the house, when you realized what fools you'd been to believe what he told you."

"How did you know—"

Tansey ignored the interruption. "So you didn't get the diamonds, and now you're up on a murder rap."

"No! We didn't murder Billy! He'd told us what we wanted to know. At least we thought— We've never killed anyone."

Tansey had the sense to remain silent once again, and at last

Ron Wilson put his head down on the desk and wept. "Oh my God!" he said. Tansey waited. The room was quiet except for Wilson's sobs and the squeak of the uniformed officer's shoes as he shifted his weight. At last the sobs subsided. Wilson found a handkerchief and blew his nose.

"It—it wasn't like you think," he muttered.

"All right," Tansey said gently. "You tell us exactly what it was like, from the beginning. But let it be the truth. We know a good deal already, and I don't want any lies. You understand?"

Ron Wilson did his best, but he didn't find it easy, and his story was far from straightforward. Nevertheless, after one or two gaps had been filled in by his sister at a later separate interview, Tansey's picture of the course of events was complete. It held no real surprises.

Billy Denville's release from prison had been eagerly awaited by his accomplices but, as Tansey knew, he had left jail a few days earlier than expected and had managed to disappear completely. Nevertheless, Turner and the Wilsons appeared to have had more perseverance than the police, and had continued to search for him after the authorities had given up. Of course the trio had not been constrained by such factors as pressure of other work, Tansey reflected.

Eventually Kay had been lucky, though she had always had at the back of her mind the proximity of Billy's father's house. Late on the day she met Billy, she had phoned Sandra Wilson. She said that Billy was posing as a parson in a village called Fairfield, and she hoped to persuade him to share the diamonds, as they had all originally agreed. She had promised to be in touch before the weekend. When she failed to keep her promise, Ron and Sandra, suspicious that they were being double-crossed, had gone to Fairfield themselves, and had seen Billy in the Church of St. Blaise.

A casual inquiry had established where he lived. When they arrived at Church Cottage that evening, he had at first tried to bluff them. They had overpowered him, bound him tightly to a kitchen chair and applied—as Ron Wilson put it—

a little pressure, in the shape of lighted cigarettes to the soles of his feet. Finally Billy had given in. He had sworn that the diamonds were in his father's house near Abingdon. They had loosened his bonds, threatened to return if he had lied and left him to meditate on these threats while he untied himself.

They had not intended to set fire to the house, or to cause his death. Why should they? demanded Ron. They were quite certain he wouldn't go to the police, and they had even promised him a small share in the diamonds.

Questioned about the Reverend Blaise Payne, both the Wilsons said separately that Billy had told them Payne had been candid enough in conversation during the drive south to make the imposture possible.

Tansey was prepared to believe them. He was happy with the events of the day. Almost all the questions had been answered. Only two remained. What exactly had happened to Kay Turner? And where were the stolen diamonds? It would give him great pleasure, Tansey thought, if he were to be the officer to hand those diamonds over to the Met.

CHAPTER 19

"But why on earth not, David?" Veronica demanded angrily.

"Because it's not done to make money from this kind of thing—the answer's as simple as that," David said. "Look, I pulled a man out of a burning house. I hope I'd try to do the same again if the occasion ever arose, though now I know the fuss the media can make about such an event I might have second thoughts next time. Anyway, the story would have died in a day if the wretched man hadn't been thought to be a parson—the nephew of a bishop, no less—and hadn't then turned out to be a phoney, a crook with a line in diamonds. I don't want to be associated with him and his activities any more."

"But no one connects you with him personally. No one connects you with his crimes. You're a hero, David, whether or not you want to be, and you'd be a fool not to cash in on it."

"Then I'll be a fool."

Veronica and David were alone in the small sitting-room at the Manor, having a drink before dinner on Friday. Sir William and Lady Gerart had not yet joined them, and no guests were expected. Bishop Payne and his secretary had left Fairfield earlier that day.

"I can't understand you!" said Veronica, her anger still evident. "You say you love me, you say you want to marry me, and you would like a shot if you had some money or any prospects. Well, here you are, being offered thirty thousand

pounds for the exclusive story of your life and how you rescued Father Payne—or Billy Whatshisname—and anything
else you know about him. It's the kind of offer you can't refuse
in the circumstances, yet you turn it down flat. You wouldn't
even have to write the damned thing yourself. Some hack
journalist would do that. All you'd have to do would be give
him an interview and let them use your name. Anyone, but
anyone, would agree to that."

"I'm not anyone. And I won't have my name splashed over
that filthy rag in order to make some money." David was by
now as angry as Veronica.

"You think you're too superior—too far above the common
herd or something—"

"Hell! I don't. I'd be perfectly happy to win a few thousand
quid on the Pools, or the Grand National—but not this way.
You'd better accept the fact, Veronica."

"It's—it's your stupid pride." Veronica was near to tears. She
was used to getting her own way, and this was one of the few
occasions on which David had put his foot down. On the other
hand, she was quite, quite sure, ever since she had been afraid
that David would die in Church Cottage, that she loved him
dearly and wanted to marry him, and no one else.

She changed her tactics. "I'm sure if we told Mummy she'd
persuade Daddy to help us," she said.

"No, Veronica! We've been through all this before, and it's
not on—not as far as I'm concerned."

"What you're really saying is that you don't love me and
you won't marry me. Isn't that right?"

David Walden opened his mouth, but choked back what he
had been about to reply. They had been so busy arguing with
each other that they had failed to hear approaching footsteps
and the opening of the door. Sir William Gerart was standing
on the threshold.

"Do I understand that you've just had the temerity to refuse
a proposal of marriage from my daughter, David?" he asked
mildly and with apparent interest.

"I wouldn't marry him if he was the last man on earth,"

said Veronica, and as the tears began to flow, she fled from the room. It might have been the last line of the first act of some kind of farce, David thought fleetingly.

"Oh dear, oh dear!" said Sir William. "Did I mishear, David, or was she right in thinking that you don't want to marry her?"

David took a deep breath. "Sir, as you know quite well, I'm completely dependent on the salary you pay me, and I'm in no position to marry anyone. I may be old-fashioned, but I'm damned if I'll get married till I am. I've been offered thirty thousand by some scandal sheet for my life story and the story of the fire, and Veronica's furious that I won't do it, just to get some capital. And I won't live off my father-in-law." He paused before he added, "Even if you would permit it. And by this time I know Veronica pretty well, and I'm sure that in the end neither of these possibilities would be a good idea. They'd be a rotten basis for a marriage, and it just wouldn't work."

Sir William nodded his head as David stared at him defiantly. Then, "I quite agree," Sir William said, "but then I'm old-fashioned too."

David heaved a sigh of relief. At least he wasn't going to lose his job. Veronica? If only he'd been cleverer or worked harder at Oxford and got a First. If only his parents had been rich or he'd inherited a large sum from a relation or a godfather or someone. If—but wishful thinking was a waste of time. It was only later in the evening that it occurred to him that Sir William had not immediately demurred at the very idea of his marriage to Veronica. In fact, in some curious fashion he and Sir William seemed to be on the same side.

Sir William was pouring himself a whisky and soda. "Forget my wayward daughter for a minute," he said. "I've a couple of items of news. First, the good. Central Office is considering possible candidates to stand at the by-election near London caused by Joe Dilland's recent death. Your name's been put forward. Of course, you'll have to meet the officers of the local association and be interviewed formally and so on, but I believe you've a fair chance of being chosen as PPC."

David was astounded. "Good God!" he said. Then he added, "But not of winning the seat, sir. It's a Labour stronghold."

"Very true, but that's not the point. Fighting a by-election—especially in a Labour-held seat—will be excellent experience for you. And if you could manage to increase our share of the vote and make a good showing, other constituencies would be after you. It's a great opportunity, David."

"Yes, sir. I appreciate that—and thank you very much. I'm sure you had a great deal to do with it."

Sir William didn't deny it. "The other news is by no means so pleasant," he said. "And it's to be kept within these four walls—though I don't see how the secrecy can last very long."

David wondered what was to come. One thing that crossed his mind was that Veronica had got herself pregnant on purpose, and then told her parents who was responsible. He dismissed the idea almost at once. She would certainly have told him first, and in any case it was the kind of ploy she'd have despised.

"The chief constable phoned me," said Sir William, and David relaxed. "He thought I ought to know that the police have obtained a coroner's order to exhume the body of Tobias Finner. The—er—the operation's to take place tonight about eleven-thirty."

"Finner?" exclaimed David in surprise. "Whatever for, sir? Surely there's not the slightest doubt that his was a natural death. For heaven's sake, Dr. Band was with him at the time."

"I've no idea why, David. But exhumation orders aren't issued casually, you know. The police must have convinced the coroner that it's an essential step." Sir William paused, and then added, "Now, as I said, not a word to anyone—including Constance and Veronica. They've had their fair share of horrors recently."

Tansey and Greenway had left headquarters and gone to Tansey's house. There they had had a leisurely drink, and Hilary had cooked them some supper. Afterwards, knowing what they would have to face later, they attempted to rest, but found it impossible. Inevitably they talked shop or fell into long silences, occupied with their own thoughts.

"If I'm wrong," said Tansey suddenly, breaking one of these silences, "the Thames Valley Police aren't going to be popular in Fairfield. Tobias Finner was a respected old man, and families, whatever their religious beliefs, are always horrified at the idea of exhuming a body after it's been safely buried."

"There *is* something awful about it, Dick."

"Yes, Hilary, I suppose there is. The chief constable probably thinks so too; I certainly had a hard enough time satisfying him that my arguments were valid, and provided a justifiable basis for action. I had to stress and stress again the importance of making sure once and for all whether the diamonds were or were not in Finner's coffin. If we found them there, I argued, one case would be closed, and everyone concerned, including possibly Tobias Finner's family, would benefit."

"But he agreed in the end?"

"Yes. Reluctantly. At least he agreed to let me apply to the coroner. Though I still don't think he believes in my theory," said Tansey.

"Then you must prove him wrong!" Hilary Greenway looked at the clock on the mantel. "It's time we were going. Come on—sir!"

Dick Tansey got to his feet and pulled her to him. "I love you," he said.

Five minutes later they were on their way to Fairfield. The cordon around Church Cottage and its immediate vicinity had been extended to include St. Blaise's Church and the churchyard. The area was patrolled by uniformed officers, and high screens had been erected around Tobias Finner's grave. This was the usual practice, though there were unlikely to be many curious sightseers on a cold February night. Indeed, it was doubtful if there was anyone present who didn't wish himself elsewhere.

To start with, the setting was eerie. It was a dark night, the cloud cover low, so that few stars were to be seen in the sky.

The moon, when it was occasionally visible, was young, a pale sliver. A light breeze sighed in the surrounding trees. But by contrast, within the high screens, floodlights fed from a mobile generator truck illuminated the grave and raised huge shadows of the small group of watchers on the screens around them.

The undertaker had already arrived, and his men had just begun digging when the chief inspector and Sergeant Greenway appeared. Inspector Colman was supervising operations with a couple of his men, and the coroner was already on the scene, with his officer. Dr. Band, as police surgeon, and the pathologist arrived almost immediately after Tansey and Greenway.

As the grave was new, and the soil had not yet compacted, the work was comparatively easy, though the men involved were sweating in spite of the cold. Nevertheless, they made good progress. A sigh went up from the huddled observers as Tobias Finner's coffin was revealed. No one, except for the inspector giving instructions, spoke.

The diggers were now deep in the grave. Two wide bands were flung to them, which they passed under the coffin. Then they scrambled out of the grave and attempted to hoist the simple pine box on to the canvas sheet spread out on the grass of the churchyard. This proved more difficult than might have been expected, and in the end the inspector detailed a couple of his policemen to lend them a hand.

Even in her padded coat, Hilary Greenway shivered as at one point in this process the coffin slipped, and nearly fell back into its grave. She glanced at Tansey and, to her astonishment, saw that he was leaning forward, eager and expectant, like a hound with a scent. If she had been asked to describe his expression, she would have said it was almost triumphant. His attitude disturbed her, but as the coffin was safely deposited on the canvas sheet he relaxed and became just another restrained watcher, more impassive than anyone.

Inspector Colman looked at Tansey. "We open the coffin here, sir? At once?"

"Yes, if the photographers are ready," said Tansey.

One of the undertaker's men was about to start to unscrew the lid of the coffin, but Tansey stepped forward and stopped him. He knelt down beside the pine box and carefully inspected the screws. Then he called the inspector and a photographer and demanded that each screw should be photographed in close-up.

"It looks to me as if this coffin's already been opened by someone who was careless or working in a hurry," he said, drawing the attention of all the observers to the minute scratch marks on the wood around the screw heads. "I doubt if a professional would have made such a mess, even on a cheap coffin." He glanced at the undertaker beside him.

"Certainly not, sir," said the man, offended. "That's not our kind of workmanship."

"All right. Go ahead now," said Tansey.

And when the screws had been undone the lid was carefully lifted from the coffin. A gasp of horror went up from the watchers, as they pressed forward to look.

The mortal remains of old Tobias Finner lay in the coffin. In death as in life he seemed a small, frail man, his frame shrunk by the many years he had lived. And jammed in beside him, as if in some obscene marriage bed, was the body of a woman, naked except for a dark blue blazer thrown over her shoulders and the chiffon scarf around her neck with which, to judge from her distorted face, she had been strangled.

"Kay Turner," said Tansey quietly. "Billy Denville's girlfriend. And that's how Denville finally got rid of Blaise Payne's blazer, with its missing button."

"No diamonds," said Greenway as they drove away from Fairfield. "You never expected them to be in that coffin, did you?"

"Frankly, no," Tansey agreed. "Though it was a perfectly plausible theory. Billy could have been facing a crisis. If he'd picked up the stones before he came to Church Cottage, or soon after he arrived here, he'd have needed to get rid of them pretty quickly once Kay had tracked him down. And you must admit it would have made a fine hiding-place. There might have been problems about retrieval, but I suspected that Billy was ingenious enough to manage the job. Anyway that's what I persuaded the chief constable."

"But why didn't you tell the chief constable you thought Kay's body was there? Because you knew, didn't you? I saw your face, and—"

"I wasn't sure, and the chief would never have agreed to applying for an exhumation order on that basis unless I had some evidence, which I hadn't. Anyway, I thought the possibility of scoring off the Met by finding their diamonds for them might appeal to him more than the off-chance of finding another body. And there is a subtle difference between merely searching a coffin for stolen goods in a churchyard, and exhuming a body for another *post-mortem* in a mortuary. Rightly or wrongly, I guessed that the diamonds were a better bet than Kay when it came to persuasion."

Hilary Greenway shook her head sadly. "You make it sound like some sort of game—arguing as if finding the diamonds was more important than finding Kay."

"They're certainly more valuable," said Tansey cynically, but he added, "Remember, there was no chance Kay could be alive."

For a while they drove in silence. It was now the small hours of the morning, it had started to rain and they were both tired after a long and trying day. Greenway was thankful that she was on her way home, unlike Inspector Colman and his men, who had been left to carry out Tansey's, the pathologist's and the coroner's instructions.

"You haven't said what made you suspect Kay was in that coffin," she said.

"Association of ideas," claimed Tansey cheerfully. "I'd been thinking how ironic it was that Tobias should have confided his dark suspicions of Colonel Brevint to the man who had actually killed Payne and buried him in Copley Wood. I thought what a terrifying moment that must have been for Denville. What if Finner had named him, the pseudo-parson, instead of Brevint? Then I thought of another bad moment that Denville had suffered, when the pall-bearer slipped on the step by the side door of St. Blaise's Church and Finner's coffin was nearly dropped. I was right beside him, and I knew that Denville's reaction was—was excessive. Suppose the damn thing were to split open, he must have been thinking."

Tansey paused, remembering the sheen of sweat on Denville's face as he had blasphemed, then tried to turn the blasphemy into a prayer.

"Then," he continued, "I remembered what Tom Cresford had said at the lunch in the crypt about the pall-bearers complaining how heavy Finner's coffin had been; they knew perfectly well that Tobias was as light as a feather. And I knew that Kay was small and would fit—or could probably be made to fit, as it were. All these ideas got together and hit me, but there was no real evidence and my combination of reasoning and intuition wasn't going to convince the chief constable. Still, he'll be pretty happy with what's happened, though I'll never be able to claim it was the result of my brilliant detection."

"But don't forget the diamonds, though I know they're not specifically our problem," said Greenway. "I wonder if they'll ever be found. And apart from the diamonds, there's another loose end—or at least a point I don't fully understand."

"What's that?" asked Tansey.

"Simply, why did Billy Denville kill Payne? What put the idea of impersonation into his head? And did he really kill a cat?"

"That's not one question; it's three. But I suspect the answers are interwoven, though I doubt if the threads will ever be totally untangled. Look, in the first place Billy was on the run. He needed to hide from the police, the insurance people and the rest of the gang, who were all anxious to discover where he had hidden the diamonds. I'd guess he was anxious to be in or around Oxford to be near his precious diamonds, though that's something we can't prove—yet. He gets a lift from the real Father Payne, who's glad to talk. Suddenly Billy realizes that here's the ideal cover for him to stick around this area. With his own background and what he's learning from Payne, impersonation should be possible, and who's going to look for a London villain in the ecclesiastical depths of rural Oxfordshire? But, to achieve this, the real Payne must be put out of the way. As far as we know, Billy Denville had never killed before. Perhaps he hesitated."

"And that's where the cat came in?"

"Well, let's assume the story was true, and not something created to explain his late arrival and his possibly slightly distraught state. It could have been the deciding factor. We know Payne had no love for animals, and was likely to take killing a cat very lightly. We also know from Billy's father about his love for a particular cat—and about his sudden bursts of temper. It's not impossible that Billy's need for a refuge and his anger coincided in some curious psychological fashion. Whatever happened, it was so much the worse for the real Blaise Payne."

Hilary Greenway said, "And once he'd taken one life, it was that much easier for him to kill Kay Turner in an unsuccessful attempt to prevent her disclosing his whereabouts to the rest of the gang."

"Right," said Tansey. "Especially as he saw such a convenient opportunity to dispose of her body."

Hilary opened her mouth to respond, but Dick Tansey forestalled her. "I know what you're going to say or hint, and I agree with you. It's a hell of a good thing we'll never have to try to prove all this in court."

CHAPTER 20

It was now Sunday again, and over a week had passed since Kay Turner's body had been found in Tobias Finner's coffin. This new sensation had revived the flagging interest of the media in the case, and it had proved a busy week for Chief Inspector Tansey, the Thames Valley Police in general and the other authorities concerned with the investigation.

Old Tobias had been reburied and Miss Mabson, who seemed to take an almost feudal interest in the Finner clan, was demanding that the family should be compensated for the distress they had suffered. She had made her views known to the press and the chief constable, but had failed to establish any source from which compensation might come—except the man—now dead—who overnight, while Tobias's coffin had rested in St. Blaise's Church, had provided him with an equally deceased companion.

The post-mortem on Kay Turner produced no surprises. As expected, she had died from strangulation with the chiffon scarf. A sister had been found to make a formal identification, the inquest had been adjourned and the body released for burial. Father Blaise Payne's body had also been released and taken north for a private funeral.

The final body, that of William Crowe Denville, reluctantly identified by his father, was still in the mortuary. Preliminary charges of manslaughter had been brought against Ronald and Sandra Wilson, who had appeared before a magistrate and been refused bail. A case against them had been prepared for the DPP, and there was little doubt that their eventual trials would result in long sentences for each of them.

The diamonds remained missing. The publicity had made sure that the insurance companies concerned had renewed their offer of a reward, but speculation as to what Billy Denville might have done with the stones was ceasing for lack of original ideas.

Neither Chief Inspector Tansey nor Sergeant Greenway was on duty this weekend. In fact, Hilary had gone off on the Saturday afternoon to visit her parents for the night, and Tansey, left to himself, had come into his office at headquarters on the Sunday morning. Having given strict orders that he was not to be disturbed unless the place was burning down, he had settled himself to prepare a full report on the progress and resolution of the Payne-Denville-Turner-Wilson case. He was doing this as much for his own satisfaction as for that of the chief constable or anyone else.

It was work he enjoyed, as long as he could proceed at his own pace, and not feel under pressure. With hindsight he often saw where he had gone wrong, where he had followed false leads, where he had missed vital clues. He looked upon the exercise as a means of improving his abilities as a police officer, and had found in the past that this kind of effort to recall all the details of a case sometimes led him to unexpected insights.

This Sunday morning was no exception. Tansey was in no hurry. He studied the files heaped on his desk, and from time to time let his mind wander idly over the events of the last few weeks.

He had, he realized, been slow to suspect that "Father Payne" was not all he pretended to be—or, rather, was more than he pretended to be—in spite of a number of indications. But the man had had such good credentials that even after his death, when it was known he had been subjected to torture of all things, it didn't seem to have occurred to anyone that he might be other than he claimed.

Suppose he had survived, Tansey ruminated. He had been alive when Walden dragged him from the cottage; both Walden and Brevint had agreed on that. Tansey turned to the relevant report, and read yet again the statements made by the two men.

Denville had probably died as he was being lifted into the Brevints' station wagon, or en route to the old vicarage. He hadn't spoken again after those few muttered words to Walden just outside the burning cottage. Tansey smiled when he remembered Walden's irritation when he had been asked about this episode.

"Dear God, I can't remember. I was lying on the ground. We were both lying on the ground. I was coughing and spluttering, and probably I didn't pay much attention to Payne at first. He was unconscious anyway, and what he said was just a mumble. I recovered my wits sufficiently to try to tell him everything was all right and help was coming, but I doubt if he understood me. Then he said something that sounded like 'anger'—or it might have been 'angst,' or something like that. Then 'no, no'—or it could have been 'crow,' perhaps. I'm sorry, Chief Inspector. I really don't know what he was on about, and frankly I don't believe he did either."

Tansey turned the page of the typescript, where all this had been translated into the more formal and stylized language of police statements. He found himself staring at the words. As before, "anger" or "angst" or "no" hadn't any apparent meaning, but now he suddenly glimpsed a possible new and different explanation for "crow." Pronounced like the bird, and typed with a small *c* and no *e*, the significance of the word had escaped his attention at the time. After all, he had then believed he was dealing with the body of Blaise Payne. But now it struck him that Billy Denville's given names had been "William Crowe."

I'm imagining things, Tansey thought. What if he did say "Crowe"? He could have known himself to be on the point of death, and wanted to make clear his real identity. But in that case why emphasize "Crowe" rather than "Denville"? On the other hand, if in his unconscious or semi-conscious state he had still imagined he was being tortured—

Tansey reached for the telephone. The obvious first step was to establish why the Reverend Edward Denville had given his son such a second name. However, there was no reply to his call, and Tansey realized that on a Sunday morning the old parson would probably not yet have returned from church. He tried Fairfield Manor.

Lady Gerart and Miss Mabson had at least temporarily abandoned their efforts to breathe life into the Church of St. Blaise, and when Tansey phoned the Gerarts were on their way, somewhat reluctantly, to a buffet lunch at the Ashes. David Walden had pleaded an incipient cold, and Veronica had simply refused to accompany her parents and had stayed at the Manor with him. Days ago she had made up her quarrel with him in a most satisfactory and satisfying manner, with the result that the two of them were now unofficially engaged with the blessing of Sir William and Lady Gerart.

Walden took a long time to answer the phone at the Manor, and his voice sounded sleepy and lazy. Tansey, who had been up since seven, had cooked his own breakfast, made his bed and gone to the office soon after eight, thought of Hilary Greenway and felt envious of Walden. It made him speak more brusquely than he might have done, but David Walden, whose mood was happy and abstracted—noises nearby explained his abstraction, Tansey thought—didn't seem to notice. Nevertheless, he was less than helpful.

"I'm sorry, Chief Inspector. Believe me, I'd have remembered if I could. Actually, it's not a question of remembering. I don't think I ever took in what he said. I told you I did wonder afterwards if it had been 'angst' and not 'anger.' But that made no more sense. Neither word seems to mean much, does it? As for the 'crow,' your guess is as good as mine, except that I agree it's odd that Denville's second name should have been Crowe."

Tansey thanked him, put down the receiver, and swore softly, as he imagined Walden getting back into bed. On impulse he tried Mr. Denville's number again and, when he was about to give up, a breathless voice answered.

Tansey gave his name and apologized for calling on a Sunday. "But there is one thing I'd like to know," he said, "and I can't think of anyone else who could tell me. It may or may not be important, but why was your son called William Crowe Denville?"

"That's an astounding question. But there's no secret about it. William after me. I'm Edward William," Mr. Denville replied. "And Crowe after his godfather, Angus Crowe, the travel writer and quite a well-known man in his line. Not that he did William any good, except for the occasional cheque, when he remembered. He's hardly ever in England, and we lost touch years ago."

This time Dick Tansey didn't swear as he replaced the receiver. He tried the words aloud, over and over again, slurring them and muttering. "Anger—no. Angst—no. Angus Crowe." He knew that he had convinced himself, though he wasn't prepared to share his thoughts with anyone else as yet. Billy Denville had called on his godfather as he was dying. Why? According to Edward Denville they hadn't been close.

The chief inspector went along to the headquarters library, and looked up Angus Crowe in *Who's Who*. Crowe was a good ten years younger than Mr. Denville. He had been educated at a public school and Oxford, and was unmarried. There was a list of his publications—seemingly serious in-depth travel works, mostly about South America. His clubs were the Oxford and Cambridge and the Travellers'. The only address he gave was that of his publishers.

Tansey was forced to be patient.

On Monday morning, Tansey, having excitedly explained his new-found hope to Sergeant Greenway, devoted himself to the telephone, fighting his way through the bureaucracy of a publishing house to track down the address of one of their authors. Eventually the managing director, with some hesitation, informed him that Crowe had an apartment in the south of France and a house in Chadlington, in Oxfordshire. He had returned from Peru a week or so ago and, after a couple of days in London, was believed to have gone to Chadlington. After further hesitation, a telephone number was forthcoming.

Trying not to be hopeful, Tansey tapped out the number. He was in luck. Crowe himself answered the phone and, when the chief inspector had explained who he was and the nature of his inquiries, at once agreed to see him later that morning.

He received Tansey and Greenway in a charming living-room, with a view overlooking lawns and gardens sloping down to a stream, with beyond that a small wood. A short, rotund man in a soft leather suit, he had eager bright eyes and a pointed beard that irresistibly reminded Hilary of a leprechaun. It was noon, and he insisted they should have a drink. He didn't ask what they would prefer, but merely rang a bell and a manservant brought in a bottle of champagne in a silver bucket with three glasses. This was clearly some form of daily ritual; Crowe was obviously rich, and did himself well.

"Poor Billy," he said. "He had plenty of talents, for acting, music and the arts generally. Not the sort of things old Edward, his father, approved of. Billy must have inherited them from his mother. But everything went wrong. Oh, I'm not excusing him, Chief Inspector. He was a bad lot, all right, but I suspect his upbringing had a good deal to do with it." Crowe shook his head sadly.

"You were his godfather, sir?" said Tansey, accepting a glass of champagne from the manservant.

"A very inadequate one, I'm afraid. I was abroad so much during his childhood. We barely kept in touch. In fact, latterly we didn't."

"When did you last see him?"

"Years ago. Before he went to prison for that damned robbery. Ingeniously planned though, wasn't it?"

Tansey made no comment on this question. He merely asked, "Can you remember exactly when, sir?"

"Remember, no. But I keep a diary and I looked it up for

you," said Crowe. "You can see the entry for yourself, if you like. It's not a real diary. Not my thoughts. Just engagements and reminders and the like. Billy turned up here out of the blue," went on Crowe, "and I have to admit he wasn't very welcome. The house was being closed for the winter because I was off to South America, and the couple who look after me were going down to my apartment in Le Cannais. Anyway, he only stayed a few hours."

"And the date, sir?"

Without hesitation Crowe produced the diary showing the date of Billy Denville's visit. It was immediately after the diamond theft, during the period when Billy Denville would have been on the run. Tansey controlled his rising excitement.

"I haven't seen or heard from Billy since," Crowe continued. "When I got back to England from that trip he was in prison. I wrote to him a couple of times, but he never answered. Then I went abroad again and—" Crowe shrugged. "That seemed to be the end of a fairly unsatisfactory relationship."

"You didn't contact the police at the time, even though you must have known we were looking for him."

"No, I didn't," said Crowe somewhat defiantly. "I'm not entirely sure I wanted to give him away. I had no desire for the publicity and in any case I was due to leave the country too soon to become involved."

"I see," said Tansey. "And it didn't occur to you to get in touch with us when you returned to England recently and learnt of your godson's death."

Crowe's smile was wry. "Frankly, no, Chief Inspector. Edward Denville's still alive. If anything needed to be done, it was up to him. I've no desire to lay claim to Billy. I wouldn't welcome the publicity any more now than I would have at the time of the crime. I'm sure you can understand that."

Tansey nodded. He wasn't prepared to make an issue of either of these points. "Now," he said, "you say you've had no contact with Denville since the day of that visit, sir. Has he by any chance tried to contact you while you were away? Say in the last several weeks."

Angus Crowe stared at Tansey. "I've only been home a few days, you know. But they tell me a man did phone, a couple of times," he said slowly. "I have no reason to believe it was Billy, but it might have been. He didn't leave a name."

Crowe had risen to his feet, and was refilling Hilary's glass. We'd better drink up quickly, before I put the next questions and he throws us out, thought Tansey.

"Sir, I have to ask you this," he said. "Is there any possibility that while Denville was here on that last occasion he had a chance to hide the stolen diamonds somewhere on these premises?"

Crowe drew himself up to his full height. "Chief Inspector," he said cheerfully, "I'm not a fool, and it's been obvious for minutes where your questions were leading. The answer is yes, of course. It's quite possible. He was here for some hours, and we weren't watching him all the time. The house is kept in excellent order, as you can see, but I take it the diamonds wouldn't be a very large packet, in spite of their value—large uncut gemstones, weren't they?—and they could well have stayed hidden somewhere, if Billy had been ingenious enough in his choice of place."

"I appreciate that, sir, but—"

"There'll have to be a search, you mean—"

"With your permission, sir."

"Or without?" Crowe gave a wide smile. "But do me a favour, Chief Inspector. Keep this business out of the papers if you can," he said. "Unless you find the damn things, of course. Then I wonder if I come in for a share of the reward."

Naturally the diamonds were discovered in Angus Crowe's house—just where Billy Denville had hidden them about eight years before. Once the ornate knob surmounting one of the hollow brass posts of a Victorian bed had been unscrewed, they were found inside.

Crowe gave the police all the cooperation they needed, but

shunned all publicity. He shut up the house again and re-treated to his apartment in the south of France. In the event, he refused any share of the reward.

The insurers were in something of a dilemma over the division of this reward, and sought the advice of Chief Inspector Tansey. He suggested that it be divided between charities and David Walden, pointing out that if Walden hadn't rescued Denville from Church Cottage, the name and relevance of Angus Crowe would never have come to light, and the diamonds might well never have been found.

But Dick Tansey and Hilary Greenway didn't go entirely unrewarded. Veronica had received from David a fine diamond engagement ring. At her suggestion a copy was made for Hilary, just before she married Dick Tansey at a quiet ceremony some months later.

About the Author

John Penn is a pseudonym which conceals a dual identity. John Penn himself was born in England and educated in London and at Oxford University. After many years of traveling widely as a government official, he turned his attention to collaborating with his wife on a series of crime novels set in London and the English countryside, that has been translated into many languages and has received considerable acclaim. American comments on previous John Penn books include "a stunning new suspense novel," "one of the best mysteries in months," "its suspense is excellent, its people engaging," "part menace, part mystery—delivered in Penn's effectively plain, straightforward style."

John Penn's wife is Palma Harcourt, the well-known author of novels of international espionage and intrigue. Together, they now make their home in Jersey in the Channel Islands.